*To: Dr. Ariston & Atty. Juliet
Ringor Clevitan,*

On World War II:

Recollections of a Young Filipino Boy

*My best wishes, Always!
Sincerely,*

by

Bibiano Arzadon y Benemerito

authorHOUSE

AuthorHouse™
1663 Liberty Drive, Suite 200
Bloomington, IN 47403
www.authorhouse.com
Phone: 1-800-839-8640

©2009 Bibiano Arzadon y Benemerito. All rights reserved.

No part of this book may be reproduced, stored in a retrieval system, or transmitted by any means without the written permission of the author.

First published by AuthorHouse 5/5/2009

ISBN: 978-1-4389-1158-8 (sc)

Library of Congress Control Number: 2008910750

Printed in the United States of America
Bloomington, Indiana

This book is printed on acid-free paper.

Names of local characters and also names of Japanese officers stationed in the Ilocos region are fictitious to avoid reopening old wounds, which had already been closed or had undergone the process of closure. Any resemblance to said characters is purely coincidental.

Acknowledgements

To my wife, Necy, on our golden wedding anniversary, who has given me the best years of my life. She inspired and encouraged me to write this book. She deserves my loud encomiums.

My deep gratitude to our daughters, Judith, Sylvia, and Eunice; to our sons, James and Sigmund; and to all their respective spouses for their understanding and great support in all my undertakings.

My appreciation to my granddaughter, Sydney, and grandsons, Aleksy, Christian, Evan, Jaysen, Justin, Neal, Simon, and Tyler, for having taught me how to grow old gracefully, which gave me happiness, vim, and a better perspective in life.

To my sister, Dr. Leonila B. Arzadon, for her daily fervent prayers for my continued health of mind and body; and to my brother Othello and his spouse for their constant moral and technical support; I am very thankful to both of them.

In loving memory of my parents, Bibiano A. Arzadon, Sr. and Felicisima Benemerito vda. de Arzadon, and my sister, Areopaguita Arzadon vda. de Evangelista and her husband Ambassador Pacifico Garcia Evangelista of the Philippines, who all have gone ahead of us in the other life, for having guided me during my formative years and for having inculcated within me the value of higher education and, above all, Christian family values.

Also, in loving memory of my deceased infant son, Spencer, who is our guardian angel.

My profound thanks to my daughter, Judith, and brother, Othello, who made the publication of this book possible.

Contents

Introduction	ix
Chapter 1 The Outset of World War II	1
Chapter 2 December 10, 1941	7
Chapter 3 December 11 to 18, 1941	15
Chapter 4 December 23, 1941	25
Chapter 5 December 24-25, 1941	33
Chapter 6 January–March 1942	39
Chapter 7 April–June 1942	49
Chapter 8 July – December 1942	55
Chapter 9 First Half of 1943	61
Chapter 10 Second Half of 1943	69
Chapter 11 January to July 1944	79
Chapter 12 August to December 1944	89
Chapter 13 Critical Days of Badoc	101

Chapter 14 　"I shall return … I have returned"	113
Chapter 15 　Reflections	119
Bibliography	125
About the Author	127

Introduction

It was 12:20 past midnight, immediately after New Year's Day, in his bedroom, where Jun was tossing, half asleep, in his bed. His wife, Gilda, snuggled close to him. He knew her face was close to his face. He felt her sweet, warm breath streaming down his cheeks.

Gilda softly touched Jun's chin in a caressing manner. Suddenly, like a metal object drawn to a magnet, she planted a kiss on his lips. He wondered why she did this as he always initiated the first move. As his mind started to ponder what her motive was, her well-rounded soprano voice softly sang, "Happy birthday to you!" He then realized it was exactly the time and day of his birth.

It was Jun's seventy-ninth birthday. It dawned upon him that seventy-nine years went by in a jiffy. It never occurred to him that he had reached almost eight decades.

He said to himself, *I cannot be this old*. After almost fifty years of a very blissful wedded life, faithful and married to the same woman, Jun still felt and acted like a man in his thirties.

So did his wife. She was svelte and always smartly dressed. When she walked, her hips swayed slightly and her whole body moved gracefully. She had a queenly look.

Since Gilda dyed her hair to medium brown to hide her gray hair, she looked twenty-five years younger than her chronological age.

Jun and Gilda were a passionate and a loving couple, blowing all their troubles away and oblivious of their surroundings when they just lazed around. On the dance floor, they were just as graceful, as romantic—*novio y novia*, gliding and waltzing to the strains of Strauss.

Pondering his age, Jun started to shudder. This petrified him. He retired from the largest inter-governmental world organization as the director for international trade (ambassadorial rank) in the Economic and Social Commission for Asia and the Pacific. He served this world organization for twenty-five years of international service, from 1960 to 1985. Prior to this, he was an economist for his government and a part-time professor of economics and statistics in one of the well-known universities in the Philippines. He also finished his contract as an adjunct faculty staff at the University of Houston Systems, teaching international business management, organization and supervision, and international marketing from 1987 to 1995. Lately, he was an international business consultant with one of the largest Japanese business firms, manufacturing valves and exporting them to all oil-producing countries of the world. After his contract with this firm ended, he was out of work. This could be the last Chapter of his active life. At his age, how could a man find gainful employment or start over with another career? Corporate America would say, "You have outlived your usefulness."

Who would hire a super-annuated person? As this thought was constantly being drummed into his head, fear of what the future will be enveloped him; and contemplating his final journey back to his creator—to the unknown—unnerved him.

As his wife went back to sleep, Jun tried to return to dreamland. He propped up his head, with his palms beneath his neck. He closed his eyes.

Then oblivion slipped in and sweet respite came in. After several hours, he started to snore. This awakened his wife.

A dim, colored light in their bedroom cast a pallid color on the face of her husband and made his body color the skin tone of a corpse, which frightened Gilda. She started entertaining morbid thoughts upon seeing Jun lying still in their conjugal bed. Those thoughts filled her with fear, reminding her of the inevitable.

As those unwholesome mental pictures overwhelmed her in the stillness of the night, a scream rung out from Jun. His body stiffened, and thereafter, he began to tremble. Beads of perspiration oozed from his forehead. Jun again had his nightmares. His wife shook him hard to awaken him.

Gilda, with a soothing voice, tried to pacify him. With her left arm engulfing him, she said, "It is all right, Jun. It is only a bad dream."

Jun suddenly woke up, gasping for breath, as if he had just reached the finish line after running a one-hundred-meter dash in ten seconds flat. Gilda inquired, "What was it this time, dear?"

Jun replied, "Some atrocities and many events during the war were unfolding in my dream; and the start of World War II was so vivid that, when reminded, I always unwittingly cower and lay down in my bed like a small child in a fetal position."

For more than six decades, almost sixty-six years, Jun had had nightmares. Sometimes he dreamt of Japanese soldiers running after him and his father, Bino, or he was a witness to the water torture treatment being given to a suspected guerrilla during interrogations by a Japanese officer. It could also be bad dreams of atrocities committed by a band of Filipino bandits and the notorious *bolo men* who dubbed themselves guerillas. Those elements took advantage of the situation during those dark days, when there was anarchy and no government, when people were running for their lives to their evacuation places, dodging bullets, caught in the crossfire of the guerillas and the Japanese soldiers.

There were even moments when such bad dreams occurred that they caused him to suddenly gather up his pillow and blanket, jump out from his bed, get out of his house, and seemingly run for his life to a distant, hidden place. More or less, he became a *somnambulist*. Those four years of Japanese regime in the Philippines and the onslaught of the so-called bolo men scarred him for life.

Those bad dreams persisted as Jun grew up. Those traumatic experiences plagued him. His various friends told him, "Why don't you tell your experiences as a young boy? Relate them in writing, and perhaps that could be a therapy to minimize the occurrences of your bad dreams." Jun acceded to such suggestions. Like a film in a reel, the episodes in his life, his recollections and reflections as a young boy riding out World War II, rolled by in this book.

Chapter 1

The Outset of World War II

It was December 7, 1942. People were terrified. Nearly every hour, the radio blurted out, "Japanese planes treacherously attacked Pearl Harbor in Hawaii. American bases in Luzon might be the next targets." People never believed such news, as their faith in the United States was unshaken.

All eyes were turned upwards, towards the north, scanning the skies for enemy planes. No droning of airplanes was heard. Only silence was felt, as if an angel had passed. Throughout the day, people were nervous, pacing back and forth, like a father would, awaiting for the birth of his first born. They were anticipating seeing a dog fight in the sky or a bomb exploding amidst them; but there was none.

In the evening, a radio commentator nervously announced, "No cause for alarm. The Japanese attacked Pearl Harbor; but they have not landed in Hawaii. Diplomatic negotiations are going on between the U.S. State Department and the Japanese Consul General in Washington, DC; hence, an impending war can be averted." This news had a very calming effect on the populace. It was pouring oil on troubled waters.

Early morning of December 8, 1941 was a great day in the Philippines; it was the feast of the Immaculate Conception. The morning bell in the school's dormitory rang merrily, ushering the coming of another day. Father Charles Bretenstein, the father prefect of the Diocesan Seminary of Neuva Segovia, who clutches and routinely rings the bell at the same time each morning, walked in between the aisles of the dormitory, where beds were lined up.

The father prefect of the seminary was the priest closest to and most involved in all affairs of the seminarians. He was actually like a foster father, looking after the welfare of all the young minor seminarians.

At night, there was the usual curfew hour at 9:30 p.m., when lights were switched off. Only the dim, colored floor lights would illuminate the darkness in the dormitory. Between 9:30 and 11:00 p.m., Father Bretenstein would walk through the aisles of the dormitory with a small flashlight—a lone, luminous small object casting its light in the black space—held in his right hand, inspecting and looking for empty beds.

As the bell rang at 5:30 a.m. the seminarians in the dormitory, although half asleep, instinctively got up and jumped to their feet. They had only a thirty-minute grace period to tidy themselves up and make their beds, taking into account the amount of time they put on their uniforms—in particular, tying their neckties in a four-in-one knot.

The dress code of minor seminarians during classes or when they went out was comprised of a pair of black shoes, black socks, white pants, black belt, white dress shirt with long sleeves (preferably with French cuffs), a black necktie, and a black blazer. If they went out for a *paseo*, they wore a flat-top straw hat, otherwise known locally as *sombrero de paja*. It was typically a very European boarding school's dress code.

Fearing that they could not make the thirty-minute grace period, they ran and rushed to the lavatory, where about one hundred bronze-colored faucets, shining in their greatest splendor, were lined up against long, white-walled tiles. They cupped their palms under the faucets and collected whatever water ran into their palms, and hurriedly washed their faces. You can just imagine the turmoil at such an early hour when about one hundred young boys would vie for the nearest faucets and cleanest places. Hurriedly, they brushed their teeth and had their oral ablutions, brushed or combed their hair, jumped into their uniforms, and rushed into the other building where the chapel was.

They had to be in the chapel at 6:00 a.m. for meditation, morning prayers, and their community mass. At 7:00 a.m., when the priest officiating the mass said, *"Ite misa est,"* the minor seminarians were ready to sprint to their assigned places in the dining room for breakfast. However, complete monastic silence was maintained from the time they got up from their beds to the end of the spiritual reading during the first fifteen minutes at breakfast. After the father prefect who read the spiritual book said, *"Tu autem Domine, Miserere nobis,"* the seminarians would answer, *"Deo Gratias,"* This was an indication that breakfast would start; and hell would break loose as the mandatory silence was broken.

Since December 8 was a holiday, breakfast was more of a feast. For breakfast, there was the ham and cheese omelet with all the trimmings, plus a slice of stuffed chicken, link sausages, mashed potatoes with gravy, and toast. The standard *calamansi* juice, chocolate, tea, or coffee were served. Bananas, peeled pomelos, sliced pineapples, *caimitos*, or star apples were also served as desserts. Instead of a rapid thirty-minute breakfast, on that day, they had an hour and thirty minutes to ingest and enjoy their food. Everybody was in a happy mood until the father prefect announced, "Pray for peace as war in China is getting more intense, and sooner or later, such war may spill over to the Philippines."

The seminarians huddled with one another, whispering to each other, "Is there a grain of truth in what the radio announced last night? Is father prefect validating the news last night?" Priests, however, were known to be good at deductive and inductive reasoning to arrive at certain conclusions.

After breakfast, the seminarians, Jun included, had to change from the standard blazer uniform into a *sotana*, surplice, and *biretta*. They had to wear the habit whenever they went to the cathedral to hear the archbishop of the diocese of Nueva Segovia say a pontifical mass in honor of the Immaculate Conception.

At 11:00 a.m., after the pontifical mass, as the seminarians walked back to the seminary, the drone of planes was heard. They were not Japanese planes but those of the American Air Force and the Philippine Air Force doing simulated dogfights as part of their maneuvers and tactical training.

At a distance, one could distinguish whether the plane was of the U.S. Air Force or of the Philippine Air Force by looking at the logo on the wings. In addition, if it was a bi-plane, it was that of the Philippine Air Force. This was a training plane and a much slower one than that of the U.S. Air Force

It was great fun to witness such simulated dogfights. It was more exciting than those shown at the movies. The seminarians were craning their necks all at the same time, following the flight of the planes. It was very interesting to note that when the planes turned to the right, their necks, at the same time, would turn to the right. When the airplanes made some dives, their knees, all together, would slightly bend downwards, following the pattern of movements of the planes.

The simulated dogfights gave them a feeling that war was imminent. The whole city was making conjectures that the Japanese were coming. But the Filipinos' faith in the United States and that it would not abandon them was strong. Within the minds of the Filipinos, the U.S. Air Force, Army, and Navy were impregnable. This fortified their spirits. This was much more so knowing full well that General Douglas MacArthur was appointed as the Commander of the United States Armed Forces in the Far East, otherwise known as the USAFE, in July 1941, by then President of the United States, Hon. Franklin Delano Roosevelt. His appointment was still fresh in their memories. The Philippine government and people had their greatest confidence in the American general. He was the adopted son of the Filipino people.

It was a common notion at that time that anything made in Japan was fragile. That being so, the Japanese tanks, airplanes, cruisers, and dreadnaughts were considered tin cans to the Filipinos. With this notion in mind, their faith in the United States was further strengthened. In fact there was a common saying in the Philippines that when someone has an upset stomach, he was told that his stomach was made in Japan. No one thought that Japan would annihilate the United States Armed Forces in Asia and the Pacific. No one expected at that time that Japan would be foremost in quality control.

Chapter 2

December 10, 1941

Late in the night of December 9, 1941, the drone of airplanes was heard coming from the northern direction of Vigan, Ilocos Sur, the venue of the Diocesan Seminary, where Jun was studying.

Vigan is the capital of the province of Ilocos Sur in the Island of Luzon. This is the seat of the provincial governor. It is situated in Northern Luzon, about twelve to fourteen kilometers from the coast of the China Sea. At that time, it was a replica of a town in Spain.

Where the seat of the provincial government was, there is at present the domed capitol. In front was a huge quadrangle, called Plaza Burgos, in honor of a Filipino priest who is one of the foremost Filipino heroes in the Philippines.

At the middle of the plaza were a fountain and a large sunken relief map of the Philippines. The map was embossed from the sunken garden, indicating all the major islands of the archipelago, namely Luzon, the Visayas, and Mindanao, with water surrounding the various islands, such as the China Sea, the Philippine Deep, the Pacific Ocean, the Babuyan Channel, the San Juanico Strait, etc.

On the left side of the quadrangle facing the capitol were the major and the minor seminaries, founded in 1611.

At the front end, fronting the capitol, was St. Paul's Cathedral. At present, it is a tourist's delight because of its painted windowpanes and frescoes depicting religious motifs lifted from the Bible. Looking at the ceiling, someone would be reminded of the Sistine Chapel at the Vatican. There is the main altar and two side altars. Along the whole length of the cathedral on both sides are numerous side altars, where newly ordained priests say their first masses all at the same time. Beside the main altar is the canopied throne of the archbishop; and at the sides, along the massive walls, are pews where the seminarians during that time sat and knelt whenever the archbishop presided or officiated.

Near the entrance to the cathedral is the belfry, with bells of different sizes to produce various tones, either in major or minor chords depending upon the bells rung at the same time or the occasion. If it were the angelus, the bells rang the toll of parting day. If it indicated a requiem mass, the bells rang the *de profundis*, or tolling of the bells. producing minor chords. If it was for a baptism, a wedding, or a feast, the bells rang so merrily. In this instance, all the bells were rung; and when they were rung altogether, they produced the major chords. For the intricate ringing of bells for all occasions, the bishop employed an experienced campanologist, which was a very rare species in the Philippines.

On the right side, facing the capitol, were the boys Catholic school for grades one to seven, the first-year to fourth-year high school, and a junior liberal arts college for both young men and women. The school was the Colegio de la Inmaculada Concepcion, run by a religious order, the Fathers of the Society of the Divine Word. Also, on the same side, facing the capitol, was the archbishop's palace, the seat of the archbishop of Nueva Segovia and his office. On the same side was also the boarding and day school for girls known as the Rosary Academy, run by the Sisters of St. Paul of Charity, a branch of the exclusive college for girls in Manila known as St. Paul's College.

Like any ancient, small town in Spain, Vigan's streets were narrow and lined with brick and concrete two-story houses and commercial buildings. Calesas, a horse drawn two-wheeled carriage, plied their trade on the narrow streets, carrying passengers from place to place. Most of the houses and buildings were of Spanish architectural design, with huge and massive brick and cement walls about half a meter thick. People there were known for being practicing Catholics or better known locally as "Catholics more popish than the pope."

The droning heard at a distance was like the buzzing of million large bees. It was indicative of a large number of Japanese airplanes flying at a distance towards Vigan. Jun became restless. Having heard over the radio and having read from the dailies of the plight of the Chinese in Mainland China, who were running away from the Japanese Imperial Army that decapitated innocent civilians and raped and tortured young and old women alike, including pregnant women bayoneted in the stomach to death, those gave Jun the shudders.

The feeling of security was already stripped from him. He feared for the lives and safety of his parents, sisters, brother, relatives, and friends. He was only thirteen years of age, but at that moment, his feelings and thoughts were matured. His empathy towards his fellowmen became stronger and more apparent. Similarly, his great faith in the United States was strong, which fortified his inner self and gave him momentary peace of mind.

That night, he was again restless and sleepless, as if he had the premonition that a great danger was lurking in the horizon. He tried to strengthen his inner self. There was a great struggle within him. Fear and courage had a bout within him. He murmured a prayer, "Lord, save us from the abyss of danger. Protect us from evil, especially from the clutches of the Japanese soldiers or anyone who harms the populace." This gave him an inner source of strength.

He was about to doze off until he heard some popping noises, like firecrackers, at a distance. His fellow seminarians assured Jun that everything was all right. They said, "The cracking and popping noises are those of the American and Philippine Armed Forces, who are doing their maneuvers and practise along the western coast of Northern Luzon."

Jun could not be pacified. He had an inkling that the Japanese were on their way to strike Manila, Corregidor, and Bataan.

At 4:30 a.m., the popping noises became more audible. Still, the belief was that the American and Philippine Armed Services were having their war maneuvers in the China Sea.

As usual, the dormitory bell, rung by Father Bretenstein, ushered in the coming of another day. Was it a joyous day or a nerve-wracking day? The daily grind of the seminarians—tidying themselves, making their beds, and running to the chapel—was duplicated on that morning. At mass, the officiating priest, Father Oppenheimer, was about to say the Kyrie Eleison, when a loud bang followed by successive short bangs and short spurts of gun shots were heard where the massive gate of the seminary was located.

The gate was likened to the then Maginot Line of France. It was thought that no human being could overrun it. It was a hard wood that seemed impenetrable, with very huge locks and iron bars embedded in the gate to fortify the wood. It was like the gates of those castles and forts in Europe in ancient times, which were of extraordinary size and of great power.

The Reverend Father Henry Burchen, a German priest belonging to the Society of the Divine Word, the rector of the seminary, rushed to the place where there was a commotion. True enough, it was at the gate. The Japanese soldiers were able to enter the front gate of the seminary, perhaps thinking that it was an army barracks. The rector, with appearance as if he was blocking them, had both arms outstretched sideways, indicating that the soldiers could not go in. He identified himself as a German priest. He shouted to the Japanese officer, "Stay where you are." The Japanese officer who led the squads of soldiers at the gate spoke English with the rector. Apparently, the Japanese officer forced his way in. They entered the seminary and inspected all nooks and corners of the building. The place they visited first was the dormitory.

Therein was Jun's cousin and classmate, named Mely. He was too lazy to go to mass in that early morning. He feigned sickness. He was left alone in the dormitory. When the soldiers entered and scoured the dormitory, they found no one except Mely in bed. They surrounded him. Their rifles, with their bayonets attached, were all pointed at him. This greatly terrified him. He was all shook up; the bed began to shake, but the Japanese started to take several steps backwards. They thought he had malaria, so they abandoned him in the dormitory. It was found out later during the Japanese occupation that ordinary soldiers thought that malaria is a very contagious disease, passed through contact. They did not know that only the anopheles mosquito with plasmodium-vivax transmits it. Otherwise, it is not that contagious through body contact.

The Japanese wanted to immediately form a military government run by civil officials but subservient to the Japanese Imperial Army. A military announcement to this effect was made. Flyers and posters announcing this great and immediate plan were pasted and posted on walls and in public places. "The whole Philippine Islands should be occupied right away and the American and Philippine Armed Forces should be annihilated and disarmed as soon as possible."

In December 10, during the day, there were some encounters against a small contingent of the Philippine Army. They were driven back to the adjoining province of Abra, next to Ilocos Sur, where tropical jungles, wild animals, and some mountain tribes existed. In Ilocos Sur, there was practically no resistance by the Philippine Armed Forces together with a few American advisers. Whatever armed resistance there was in Ilocos Sur during that period was symbolic.

In Central Luzon, however, radio broadcasts indicated that the first wave of Japanese soldiers were like flying white ants that flung themselves into a burning kerosene light and all were killed. While the Philippine and American Armed Forces retreated slowly towards Bataan and Corregidor, their last bastion, wave after wave of advancing Japanese soldiers were annihilated. They really fought bravely and died for the cause they believed in. This was a manifestation of the fervor, loyalty, and love they had for their country and their emperor, which was very obvious and unmistakable.

With Japanese armored vehicles rolling over flat and undulating terrains, and zero planes hovering above to give protection to the battalions and battalions of Japanese soldiers, the American and Philippine soldiers retreated but put up a good fight. Many dispersed, and many Philippine Army units were disbanded. Most of those were college students, under the ROTC program, who were recruited or volunteered to join the armed forces. Many of those soldiers immediately buried their arms and discarded their uniforms. Many of them, in only their underwear, sought cover in the jungles nearby and started going home on foot.

In Ilocos Sur, where resistance was minimal, as noted earlier, those who were wounded or captured were herded like animals towards Manila, while those who were able to retreat went farther into the jungles of Abra and Mountain Province to regroup. Those who were too weak to move on with their captors or already in the brink of death, which impeded the fast pace of the Japanese Imperial Army's advance to victory, were bayoneted or shot to death on the spot by the Japanese soldiers.

The Filipino civilians in Vigan stayed indoors. They were afraid of the Japanese soldiers because of what they had read in newspapers and magazines or heard over the radio about the atrocities they inflicted in China. What they could do at the outset of the war was only to peep out their windows, very curious to see what the Japanese soldiers were doing.

Chapter 3

December 11 to 18, 1941

In the days that followed, there were some sporadic attacks outside Vigan, Ilocos Sur, where the Japanese were believed to be encamped. Between midnight and the early morning, the U.S. Air Force and the Philippine Air Force, locally dubbed the night raiders, used to drop their light bombs and spray the Japanese soldiers with bullets from machine guns mounted on their airplanes. Tracer bullets would light up the skies, and the pounding sound of anti-aircraft guns could be heard at a distance. During such missions, sometimes stray bullets found their way inside the town of Vigan, and this greatly petrified the populace.

Despite the few American and Philippine planes that flew, they were able to inflict some casualties to the Japanese Imperial Army. They were dropping bombs and spraying bullets in a very concentrated area full of Japanese soldiers. However, to the Japanese, by the theory of numbers, the casualties were not significant at all. As days went by, fewer and fewer intermittent attacks by the night raiders were made until the skies were freed from marauder attacks.

The minor and major seminary continued operating as a boarding school exclusively for first- to fifth-year minor seminarians, the first two years of philosophy, and the four-year theology course for major seminarians, which were the required courses before one was ordained as priest. The first- to fifth-year minor seminary course was the equivalent of an American general high school, comprised of the general academic courses, with the addition of English, Latin, Spanish, Tagalog, Nippongo, religion, and the humanities.

Food supplies, however, dwindled to a bare minimum as people and farmers evacuated to far-flung areas in the tropical jungles, where wild boars, poisonous snakes, mosquitoes with plasmodium vivax, and amoebic dysentery bacteria abound. Cash crop plantations, rice farms, vegetable gardens, pig farms, and poultry farms were abandoned and neglected; hence, farm production was practically nil. Seminarians, therefore, were told to go home temporarily until a better situation prevailed.

Mely and Mady, both seminarians and classmates of Jun, decided that they should trek back to their hometown, Badoc, Ilocos Norte. It is the first town of Ilocos Norte going northbound from the national highway from Ilocos Sur. It is a smaller town than Vigan but with the same layout.

At the center of the town was the town plaza, with an open auditorium and theater bounded by the municipal hall at one end. On one side was the elementary school. The opposite side was the small emergency hospital. In front of the municipal hall was the Catholic church, which at that time was about two hundred and fifty years old. On the right side was a private high school, the Juan Luna Memorial Academy, for boys and girls.

The municipality is one of the oldest towns in Ilocos Norte and has produced very fine professionals, especially in letters, music, arts, and sciences. It has produced national figures, such as ambassadors, members of the house of Congress, high civil servants, university professors, and corporate executives. The most prominent son of the town was Juan

Luna y Novicio, the foremost Filipino painter, who won world acclaim for his painting, *The Spolarium*. It was a prizewinning piece of art, a first prize winner in a competition held in Europe. It was exhibited in Madrid in the late 1800s. The other was his brother, General Antonio Luna, a Filipino hero who fought for independence against the Spaniards.

Badoc was more of a fishing and farming town. It is nestled along the coast of the China Sea, with the Cordillera Mountains in the background. It has the most beautiful sunsets in the country, where the blood-red sun sinks in the western horizon and the luminous afterglow slowly blends with the darkness of the night. No doubt, the Japanese, always in harmony with nature in war or in peace, loved this town.

The three young seminarians, all thirteen years of age, were looking forward to reaching their beautiful hometown and being with their own families on or before Christmas or before New Year's Day. They went to bid good-bye to their reverend father rector; they knelt before him while he gave them his blessings. He said a short prayer for them for their safety. The boys, one by one, kissed the right hand of their rector before they stood up and departed from his office.

Similarly, they went to their father prefect, who also gave them his blessings and prayers. He hugged them like a parent would to his own sons. The father prefect whispered to them in a prayer, "May God bless you and protect you on your way."

The boys waved at their fellow seminarians once they departed and passed through the massive gate of the seminary. They never looked back, as they had heavy hearts upon leaving. They had mixed feelings: sorrow silhouetted with happiness; sorry to leave, but happy to soon be with their own families.

They passed through the massive gate at seven o'clock in the morning of December 17, 1941.

They had to hike to the main highway heading northbound, as there were no transportation facilities. Only the Japanese military trucks were rolling on the road.

Each of the boys carried a laundry bag full of his few personal items, with some peso bills in his pockets.

They had no untoward incidents with the Japanese soldiers; but in San Ildefonso, Ilocos Sur, a town north of Vigan and Bantay, Ilocos Sur (a town adjacent to Vigan), a crowd of drunken men held them up. The hoodlums took all their money, including all the food they carried. They were divested of food, drinks, money, and some of their personal items. The three boys pleaded to them, "We are young seminarians going back to our parents. Please do not take our food items. You can have our money, but please give us back our food. We have nothing to eat on our way. We are just kids."

The drunken men turned a deaf ear. Instead, they told the three young boys, "Run for your lives."

The boys, frightened, took off as fast as they could; they heard the laughter of those bad men and never turned to look back. What was disgusting was that those adults took advantage of those young boys at a time of adversity.

While trekking, the three young seminarians were getting dehydrated. They were suffering from hunger pains, especially when the sun was almost vertical over their heads. Mely was beginning to have cramps in his left leg. Mady started to cry for fear that somebody on the way might waylay them all. Jun told them to build up courage. He yelled at the two and said, "Stop being sissies. Do not act like five-year-old kids. Have faith in the Almighty and we shall get through these tribulations."

They tried to get into some houses at random along the highway to ask for water or food, but they were all deserted. The towns that they went through were ghost towns. Not a single person except for a few dogs could be seen. The three young boys had been to some eerie places.

Suddenly, they heard engine noises. Their hearts leaped with fright. True enough, it was a convoy of Japanese troops going in the opposite direction. The last truck stopped where other Filipino young men were herded. Where the young men came from, the seminarians had no inkling at all.

Jun, followed by Mely and then Mady, was yanked into the truck by a Japanese officer. The Japanese officer spoke impeccable English with a British accent. He told them to obey everything they were commanded to do; otherwise, all of them would be punished accordingly.

The three young ones, trembling with fear, were shoved into the truck. Together with some forty young boys, all high school students, they were taken to an unknown destination. They were all picked up on the national highway like the three seminarians on their way back to their parents. They were packed in the truck like sardines in a tin can. Their apprehensions were so great. All of them had the greatest trepidation and fear of the unknown.

The truck was going back to Vigan; but they stopped in a Japanese camp set up between Bantay, Ilocos Sur, and a picnic area, called Caniao. The fears and apprehensions of the three young ones were a little bit assuaged as the location was a very familiar one.

The minor seminarians used to go there for picnics and swimming. The place was very scenic, overlooking the Banawang River, rapidly flowing towards the China Sea. This river was used as a waterway for logs and agricultural produce from the province of Abra, like a middle finger of the China Sea cutting two fjords covered with green grass, majestic trees, and other verdant growths, with a suspension bridge spanning the two. Looking from a distance and going over the bridge was a breathtaking experience.

Why they were brought there was a sixty-four-dollar question to the forty young men. The conjecture and speculation within their minds petrified them, such as, "Are we going to be executed in a killing field?" All the young boys would try to escape if they had a chance.

A part of the Japanese convoy forked out and proceeded to Vigan, while the tail of the convoy, including the truck where the young ones were jam-packed, went near the picnic place. There was a plateau near the river where a tent was pitched. It was a temporary barracks for the Japanese soldiers.

The young students were told to alight from the truck and form a line, four deep. They followed the orders quite well.

The Japanese officer, who spoke English with a British accent, told them that they were there as a working crew to build a makeshift landing strip for their single-motored reconnaissance airplanes. He informed them that if everybody worked hard without any letup, the makeshift airstrip could be finished in five working days.

The officer warned them with a stentorian voice, with his right hand holding the handle of his sword, "Do not escape. If one does, all of you will be punished accordingly." This agitated the boys with great anxiety about the many dangers ahead.

The young boys looked around and murmured to one another, "Where is our food and water? Where shall we sleep? We do not have pillows, mats, or blankets. Shall we sleep under the canopy of the sky, with the stars twinkling at us?" Those were their minor concerns. The major ones, they harbored them within their minds.

The Japanese officer then told them, "You will start clearing the area tomorrow and then construct the airstrip. In the meantime, you will go to Vigan to sleep, as there are no sleeping facilities here."

The Japanese military police had their headquarters in Vigan at the old Luzon Hotel, which was just a stone's throw from the dormitory of the seminary.

The young boys slept in the *sala* or living room of the hotel. They had no beddings, but at least they had a roof over their heads and were not exposed to the vagaries of nature.

For dinner, the Japanese handed the boys balls of rice, with dried seaweeds, dried fish, and raw eggplants, followed with a glass of water as a chaser. The boys, not used to the taste, forced themselves to swallow the seaweeds and fish. They were not accustomed to eating salted, sweetish food and raw eggplants. At least the food was filling. This was the typical food of Japanese soldiers at the beginning of World War II.

At 6:00 a.m. on December 18, 1941, a Japanese sergeant awakened the boys. They were lined up outside and marched to the plaza in front of the hotel. They were told to face the east, where the sun would rise, and bow their heads towards the direction of the Japanese emperor and pay respects to him. They were taught how to bow the Japanese way. It was a novelty to the boys. The Japanese were happy to see how fast the boys learned.

After a few minutes, a Japanese soldier came forward and spoke in English, telling them to follow his instructions and command. He told them to learn the *radio taisho*, a form of calisthenics.

The boys easily learned it. In school, they were taught calisthenics as part of their physical education course. They found out that radio taisho is almost similar to what they learned in school. The Japanese mentor was greatly pleased at how the boys executed the instructions with ease. They also learned how to count in Japanese, from *ichi, ni, san, shi, go, roku, shichi, hachi* to *hachi, shichi, roku, go, shi, san, ni, ichi*. This is the cadence of the radio taisho, which in English is from one to eight and from eight to one.

The young boys and the Japanese *sensei* (the teacher), as well as the Japanese officer, had mutual feelings of satisfaction about the accomplishment they had made in so short a time.

As a prize, the boys were given a substantial breakfast, taking into account that those were the first days of the Japanese occupation, when food was lean.

Below the hotel was a Chinese bakery. The Japanese ordered the Chinese baker to prepare hot *pan de sal*, similar to the Spanish bread, with a crispy and hard crust but in a smaller size, like the fist of a boy.

Coffee was served, along with the hard-boiled *tamago*, the hard-boiled eggs. In wartime, hard-boiled eggs were the easiest food to prepare.

Having two or three pieces of *pan de sal* filled the stomachs of the boys and gave them that heavy feeling. The boys were satisfied and were ready to go to the work camp.

After breakfast, they were again herded into a truck; and off they went to the construction place.

Armed with wheelbarrows, spades, forks, rakes, and crowbars, the boys were marched into the open field and started digging, leveling the ground, and placing some sub-soil and gravel from the river bed nearby. Then a steamroller engine was brought from Vigan to level off and smooth the naked strip.

The boys, because they were in the same age group and from the same province, without any cultural differences, were very compatible with one another. They grouped themselves into four teams of ten.

One team was the digging squad. The other was the carrier squad, which carried the sub-soil and gravel, in wheelbarrows, from the riverbed to the dug portions of the ground. The third team was the filling squad, which spread out the sub-soil and gravel placed on the ground. The fourth team was the leveling squad, which followed the steamroller engine and smoothed out the surface and let it harden by placing asphalt on it.

There was specialized labor by teams, but as a whole, there was synergy. There was a great lesson learned by the boys here. The four individual teams, taken in the aggregate as one team as opposed to an individual group approach, attained greater production efficiency. This was their first lesson in production economics. The spirit of cooperation among the teams, working as one, was greatly emphasized to produce results.

In view of the spirit of cooperation and the synergistic approach undertaken by the forty boys, it took them only four days to finish the landing strip instead of the planned five-day period. Because of the hard work done by the boys and the good results, they were rewarded with *Akebono* (Japanese cigarettes), Japanese medicines, and a lot of seaweeds which Filipinos also eat with gusto when eaten like a salad with tomatoes, salt, and vinegar, or mixed with *sinigang*, a Filipino dish.

In addition, the boys were given a one-and-a-half-inch-wide white strip of cloth, like a ribbon, with the rising sun's emblem. Their names, ages, and places of residence were written with Indian ink on the ribbon, in *kanji, hiragana,* and *katakana* (the Japanese alphabets and characters), like an identification card. The signature of the Japanese officer was conspicuously written at the bottom of the white strip of cloth. This strip of cloth became an identification card and a certificate of good conduct.

That ID was pinned at a vantage point in front of a shirt or blouse. This ID gave the boys a pass to enable them to go through any Japanese sentry without being summarily accosted and inspected or humiliated. Japanese sentries were terrors during those days.

The news of the good treatment given to the young boys spread like wild fire in the Ilocos region. It became propaganda of the Japanese

Imperial Army. This caused the local people to gain confidence in and a feel more comfortable with the Japanese.

It was said that the Japanese convoy that herded the young students for construction work was a contingent of the Propaganda Corps of the Japanese Imperial Army. The officers and soldiers of the corps were strict but disciplined and courteous, and observed protocol.

Chapter 4

December 23, 1941

Since the newly constructed landing strip was about twelve kilometers away from Vigan, the forty young boys were whisked back to the hotel every night, when the day was done, for their night's rest.

December 23 was the inauguration of the newly constructed landing strip. The Japanese top brass and the other officers belonging to the higher echelon were there. The flag of the rising sun was hoisted; the bowing of the heads towards the east, the direction of the sunrise and the symbolic direction of the emperor of Japan, was observed.

The three seminarians and the rest of the young boys similarly followed the observance of the flag-raising ceremony and the bowing of the heads towards the direction of the seat of the emperor. After those ceremonies, the Japanese soldiers gave a thunderous applause. The young boys felt guilty about what they had accomplished, knowing full well that what they had done would certainly advance the war efforts of the enemy and may cost the lives of their Filipino brothers. They were not able to do otherwise because they had to save their own lives. They had to obey what the aggressors commanded them to do. They were simply helpless.

With their arms pumped upwards, the Japanese soldiers exclaimed, "*Banzai, banzai, banzai,*" which rang in the air. It was a sign of victory or of great accomplishment. The young ones, much against their will, followed suit for fear that their anti-Japanese emotions might betray them.

The Japanese officer with the British accent took a step forward, saluted his commanding officer, and addressed the young boys. He announced with great authority, "The Japanese Imperial Army had their forces land at Lingayen Gulf yesterday, which was the 22nd of December, 1941. The massive offense of the Japanese forces rendered the Philippine-American forces totally ineffective. All the resistance was overwhelmed by the blitzkrieg attack of the Japanese Imperial Forces." With those remarks, the boys' feelings of defeat caused their heads to hang loosely from their necks, with very heavy hearts.

The Japanese officer further addressed the boys. "In the name of the Japanese Imperial Forces, I commend you for the work you have done for us. You can go home now, spend your Christmas and New Year's Day with your loved ones. Tell your people that we, the Japanese Imperial Forces, are here to liberate you from the clutches and chains of the American imperialists." Upon hearing this remark, all the boys again had a guilty feeling that what they had accomplished would aid the enemy.

The Japanese officer moved forward and shook the hand of each boy. He ordered the driver of the truck to transport the young boys northbound, together with another truck full of soldiers, as vanguard, with machine guns mounted at the top of the driver's seat.

While doing the construction work, the boys developed camaraderie. They became close friends overnight; and they had that sense of belonging with one another. As they departed, they hugged each other and made a promise that they would seek out each other when better days were there again.

Both trucks rolled northbound from the landing strip, in the same direction from which the forty boys were picked up on the way. As the truck proceeded to the north, each of the boys told the driver to stop where they were to be dropped off. Normally, it was in the vicinity of their respective hometowns.

Jun, enjoying the scenery on both sides of the national highway, started to see familiar landmarks as they neared the boundary of the provinces of Ilocos Sur and Ilocos Norte. He was getting excited, as were Mely and Mady.

When the truck wound its way down the zigzag road towards Ilocos Norte, at a distance, in bold letters, Jun read at the top of a concrete arch, "Welcome to the Province of Ilocos Norte." He shouted with glee, "I am home! I am home." The Japanese soldiers who accompanied them also clapped their hands with approval.

The three seminarians got down beside Jun's house. Without sparing a minute, the two Japanese military trucks went farther northbound to drop off the remaining young boys.

Jun's house seemed deserted. Not a single soul was seen. Japanese trucks seldom went by inside the town. If people heard an engine noise of a truck at a distance, they ran to their hiding places until they heard the truck had left. If they thought that the truck was already kilometers away from the town, that was the sign that all was clear. It was only then that they ventured out and continued with their normal chores.

When the engine noises of the two trucks could no longer be heard, the few people who were left behind in the town slowly appeared, one by one, until they converged into a crowd. With great astonishment and joy, they received their favorite three young boys, safe and sound in their midst.

Jun, with his naked eyes—his spectacles encased and neatly kept in his back pants pocket—was able to pinpoint his father. One could not miss him, as Bino's hair had prematurely turned silver a number of years ago. The silver temple stood out amongst black-haired people in a crowd. It was like a sore thumb sticking out from a hand.

Jun rushed to his father. With arms outstretched, Bino caught his son, engulfing the young boy, and gave him a tight embrace.

The time had come for Mely and Mady to leave. Their relatives, who were a part of the crowd that converged when they arrived, brought them to their respective evacuation places. Tears welled from Jun's eyes as they said good-bye to one another. Bino gave a big hug to his nephews Mely and Mady, and wished them Godspeed.

Hand in hand, father and son strode up the concrete stairway of their house. As they were going up, Jun's hands clasped his father's right hand tighter and tighter as they took one step at a time. This gave the young boy a feeling of security, being near his father. He had missed his father very much, because Bino had not visited his son in the seminary for almost six months.

Being alone together brought joy to the two. Happiness was infused into their bloodstreams. There was peace and quiet when they sat together on a rocking, reclining chair, commonly called, *butaca*. That was the same chair where they sat on together when Bino used to tutor Jun in mathematics as a young boy. Jun reminisced about those happy childhood days when father and son used to sit together on that same butaca.

All of a sudden, the drone of airplanes was heard at a distance. When they looked out the windows, the rising sun emblems were conspicuous under the wings of the Japanese airplanes. They were in a V-shaped formation, with several planes on both sides of the formation. The airplanes were headed towards the south, presumably going towards Bataan, Corregidor, and Manila.

What Bino and Jun saw in the sky, coupled with the drone of airplanes, disturbed the engaging moment between father and son. They were enjoying each other's company, offsetting those lost days, weeks, and months when Jun was away at school.

Jun's father prepared a sumptuous lunch for his son. Bino cooked Jun's favorite soup, the *Tinola*; the main dish, *Adobo*; and the viand, *Dinengdeng*. That lunch seemed fit for a king after those days of compulsory diet food at the work camp.

After two hours of rest, Bino told his son, "Sonny, you have to go to the evacuation place, which is twelve kilometers away from the town. Your mother had many sleepless nights, crying out for you because she did not know your whereabouts. Your brother and sisters are all there in my farm, staying in our tenant's house. They will be most happy to see you."

Jun understood his father. It was much against his will to leave him. He wanted to be with his father through thick and thin. Those were his true feelings.

Agustin, a relative of the family, accompanied Jun to the evacuation place, called Padung-ar. It was a large farm devoted to farming rice, maize, and sugar cane, as well as truck gardening, which produced wide varieties of vegetables and fruits, such as bananas, pineapples, and mangoes.

They went over hills and traversed rice paddies and cornfields, thick banana and mango plantations, and crossed brooks to reach the evacuation place. Those were hurdles that impeded their progress in reaching their destination. It took them more than five hours to reach the farm.

The tenant's house was large but hidden from above by branches of large mango, acacia, and eucalyptus trees, which grew majestically upwards, as high as can be. This gave them a vantage point for an evacuation house. Its roof was camouflaged by the branches of trees, like tentacles of a giant octopus. This prevented flying enemy planes from spotting the house. The place could only be seen by low- and slow-flying scout planes if there was a flickering light on a dark night or dark smoke curling up to the sky from a kitchen on a clear day.

Jun's steps became slower and slower. His legs started to cramp. His heart beat faster and faster. His breathing became harder and harder. He was hyperventilating as they reached the vicinity of the evacuation place.

Agustin, looking at the tired and haggard boy, cracked jokes with him to buoy up his spirits. He motivated him to forge on by telling him, "Go on, young man, your mama, brother, and sisters can now be seen at a distance, all lined up at the window sill." No one was seen at a distance. It was only a joke. He further chided him by saying, "Can you see what I see?" Those were only some of his jokes to motivate him to go forward.

It was by chance that Jun's brother and sisters, while enjoying the panoramic view of the fields, trees, and clouds above rolling by, spotted a man and a boy balancing themselves while walking at a very narrow path along the rice paddies.

As the two figures were drawing near, the children immediately recognized the two. They ran outside, shouting, "Jun is here; Jun is here with Uncle Agustin."

His mother, Fely, upon hearing the excitement outside, did not believe what was happening. She ran out, and what she saw afar was incredible. She silently said to herself, *Am I looking at a vision, or is it real?* As Agustin and Jun were about fifty meters away from the house, Fely, unconsciously rubbing her eyes, apparently to clear her vision, finally believed what she saw. In front of her was a son who grew up to five feet seven inches tall. He was barely five feet tall when she saw him last. Also, when Jun greeted her and said, "Mama," he had a raspy voice, a changed voice that was deep and an indication that he had reached the age of puberty.

Fely rushed to him, as a mother would to a son whom she had not seen for quite some time. She kissed him once, followed by another, and then showered him with innumerable kisses. The sisters and brother joined in, in a huddle, with Fely at the center. She asked everybody to join her in prayer of thanksgiving for delivering her son from harm.

Fely went to the kitchen to prepare dinner and to boil water to pour into a half- full tank of cold water outside for Jun to bathe himself. Jun had to dip his hands in the water to test the temperature. It was just right. It was lukewarm. The bathroom was enclosed with bamboo walls made out of bamboo slits. There were no tiles, but one had to stand on four square feet of stone mined from a quarry, on bare ground. There was no ceiling. Only the bright sky canopied the makeshift bathroom.

There was no shower at the bathroom—no running water either. Instead, there was the pitcher and catcher system. The catcher was the tank to hold the water drawn from the well; and the pitcher was the pail that poured the drawn water into the tank. This was how Jun bathed himself, taking a polished coconut shell to scoop the water from the tank each time he poured water over his head and body. The lukewarm bath eased his aching muscles after a long hike and induced him into a deep and restful slumber after dinner.

It was already dark. Nighttime had just set in. Fely was about to finish cooking for dinner, but instinctively, she got a jar full of water, poured it hurriedly over the firewood, and extinguished the fire. She did this on time, as if a hidden power had just pulled her arms to do so. Low-flying enemy planes had been heard overhead, circling around like a hawk searching for its prey.

As the fire was extinguished, heavy smoke went up through the spaces of the woven bamboo slats, which served as kitchen walls. Fely did not panic because smoke curling up at night was not visible anyway. It was only the flying cinders or any luminous object or any flickering light that would have betrayed their position. This was one of their first lessons in keeping one's position a secret. Because of the scout planes, the fire was extinguished before she finished cooking. Hence, they all ate half-cooked food for dinner. The beef, however, was so good because it was medium-rare.

Again, they heard the Japanese planes circling above. They had to make sure that the lights were extinguished. Everybody was nervous, waiting for a bomb to explode or the rattle of machine guns spurting bullets. The feeling of anxiety was nerve-wracking. Jun's body was as cool as a cucumber while his palms were sweating. After a short while, the roar of planes was no longer heard. A general feeling of relief lingered all night long.

Chapter 5

December 24-25, 1941

After a very early breakfast on the 24th of December, Fely assembled her children for a family caucus. She asked everybody's opinion about whether the whole family would go to town and be with their father at Christmas Eve and possibly hear mass on Christmas Day.

The parish priest, Father Florentino, stayed behind and did not evacuate at all. He stood pat in his parish to minister to the needs of his parishioners and to give spiritual support to those who were left behind in the town. For sure, there was mass on that Christmas Day.

A consensus was reached that they all should join their father, whom they had not seen for days.

Fely prepared some food for Christmas that they could carry to town. She planned to cook the main dish in Badoc, where she would have all the ingredients in the kitchen and all the utensils needed. In the evacuation place, they did not have all the paraphernalia needed and the desired ingredients.

Fely had one problem: the safety of the children, especially the daughters. She was scared that there was no good place to hide when crossing the national highway. They might encounter a Japanese truck or convoy at the crossroad.

Everybody was stumped by this problem. Right at that moment, Jun thought of the strip of white cloth on which his name, age, date of birth, and place of domicile were written in Japanese characters and signed by the Japanese officer below the logo of the rising sun. It was officially given to him by the Japanese Imperial Army as his ID, certifying that he was a person of good moral standing and of good conduct. He paused for a moment, trying to remember where he had stashed it. He finally tried looking in his trunk. There it was, lying on his watch case. He took it and pinned it on the breast pocket of his shirt. He proudly showed it to his mother, brother, and sisters, to everyone's astonishment .

He told them, "This strip of white cloth enables us to have safe passage to town. No Japanese will ever lift a finger against us. They will respect this strip of cloth." There was credence in his voice. His statement built courage within himself to venture to town. They mustered enough courage to go through that crossroad on which everyone feared to tread.

They finally embarked on their planned hike to town. They were so careful that they all walked single file, at least fifty meters apart from each other. This would give each person a chance to run or seek cover elsewhere if the forerunner was captured first. This was only a precautionary measure.

It was a great sight to see them in single file, balancing on a very narrow path along the rice paddies. They moved like acrobats on a very narrow plank of wood at great heights, bridging a raging river below. Upon reaching the much-feared crossroad at the national highway, their hearts pounded hard. Their ears were kept wide open to hear any engine noise. They heard nothing except their heartbeats and their swishing footsteps across muddy terrain. They ran as fast as they could until they felt they were already in the threshold of safety. They also had a feeling of security because of the white strip of cloth, which Jun had pinned on the lapel of his shirt.

They finally reached their residence in Badoc, past mid-day. Although it was December, they were all sweating under the scorching sun in the humid tropical climate.

Bino was greatly surprised and pleased to see his whole family at Christmas. It was beyond his expectation that they would be there. The three children saw the great happiness expressed by his eyes. There was even a smile in his voice. He had not seen his family for a number of days, and above all, he missed his charming wife.

He gave a passionate kiss to his wife first; then he gave a paternal embrace to the children. It was such a beautiful picture of a family reunion in a war-torn zone.

Jun noticed that as his father looked at his wife, Fely, a faint blush rushed to his father's face and his breathing became a little bit heavier. He even understood what the eyes of his father meant. Those eyes, burning with desire, had that ravishing look after the absence of his mother from their conjugal bed. The children, being so understanding, gave their parents a chance to be together.

They went to church to pray in the evening, as there was no midnight mass on that Christmas Eve. The parish priest was very happy to see the four children, especially the seminarian. He assured them that there would be a Christmas mass at 8:00 a.m. on Christmas Day. Father Florentino said if there were a great number of people at the service, "I will have a *misa cantada* or a high mass."

Most people returned unexpectedly to the town on December 25, 1941, just to hear mass. Jun's elder sister, Ariana, who was an accomplished pianist, played on the organ as an accompanist. His sister, Lea, who turned out to be a dentist and science teacher, joined the choir. Most of the choir members were also present. Jun, as a seminarian, served the mass. Bino, Fely, and Lito (the youngest in the family, who later in life became a chemist and a medical technologist) sang Christmas carols with the congregation and the choir with all their hearts' content.

Outside, there was some commotion, which slightly disturbed the solemnity of the mass. There was the screeching of brakes of trucks at the compound of the church when the mass was almost over.

The priest, towards the end of the mass, had to turn towards the congregation to give his last blessings. In doing so, his eyes caught the truckloads of Japanese soldiers coming in through the aisles, towards the altar.

The sight made the priest's blood ran cold. The congregation was benumbed and filled with fear. On the other hand, they never let their emotions run astray.

Those soldiers coming into the church were the same unit that picked up the boys to construct the makeshift airstrip in Ilocos Sur and the same ones that transported them back to their respective homes.

Since Jun always pinned the white strip of cloth with the Japanese emblem on the front of his shirt, he dauntlessly met the soldiers. He boldly faced them because of the previous assurances of safety given by the Japanese officer that whenever he visibly wore the badge, he would be treated as a good citizen of the community.

The Japanese soldiers observed the decorum in the church with all the solemnity, piety, and dignity accorded to a place of worship. They smiled at the young seminarian when they saw his ID pinned on his shirt. The whole congregation, including Bino, was amazed at the behavior shown by the soldiers.

The Japanese officer approached Father Florentino and sought permission to make an announcement to the congregation. The priest could not refuse and had to accede to the Japanese officer. The officer took several steps forward and stood immediately in front of the communion rail. He spoke and broke the news. "Yesterday, which was the 24th of December, 1941, your General Douglas MacArthur abandoned you. He retreated in defeat and is now hiding in Bataan or being entrapped in Corregidor. Also, your government declared Manila an open city, which the Japanese Imperial Army has carefully observed to prevent civilians from being annihilated and buildings from being bombed. This means that your government has abandoned you. Now, you better cooperate with us, and we will liberate you from the clutches and chains of the United States."

The people of Badoc, deep within their hearts, never believed what they heard. They kept in mind that those words were spoken between the teeth. They were all propaganda. On the other hand, it was later found out that Manila was declared an open city and that General MacArthur went to Corregidor, an island and an underground city. The Filipinos believed at that time that Corregidor was as impregnable as the Maginot Line of France.

That Christmas Day was the first time the citizens of Badoc had an encounter with Japanese soldiers. They observed those Japanese as a bunch of disciplined and courteous soldiers observing protocol. Like a two-faced chip, with a white color on one side and a red color on the other side, the desirable side was shown.

After that, people went back and forth from the town to their evacuation places. They freely went to their farms, without any impediments, to get their produce to town for sale or for their own consumption. A bit of normalcy was returning to Jun's hometown.

After mass, Bino and his family all went back to their house. Christmas brunch was prepared and served by Fely. Being the head of the family, Bino gave an after-dinner short talk to grace the occasion, which was the custom of the Filipinos. With utmost sincerity and humility, he told his family, "On this Christmas Day, I have no presents to give to each of you. All what I can offer you is my love and devotion. Your presence today is my most precious gift from you."

After that short remark, they all joined hands and praised the Lord for all the gifts and blessings showered upon them. To them, the whole family together on that occasion, when no one expected to see the light of another day, was a day to remember for a lifetime.

Chapter 6

January–March 1942

Bino came running from nowhere. His face was ashen. Fely and the children had an inkling that something was wrong. Bino, with his voice shaking, said, "My greatest concern and fear has finally come. The Japanese forces already occupied Manila." This was on January 2, 1942. Manila fell on Jun's fourteenth birthday. This was a *bolo punch* to the family. There was no birthday party for Jun.

Bino continued to relate what he heard over the clandestine radio. "Manila was declared an open city on December 24, 1941. Declaring Manila as such was to prevent destruction of the whole city and the populace. This makes me feel good, as no civilian was hurt or building destroyed." The Japanese forces entered Manila as free as the wind that only makes the leaves rustle and the dried ones fall.

The Filipinos, with a heavy heart, had to swallow their pride. Their faith in the United States, however, never faltered. On the other hand, further patriotism on the part of the Filipinos was sparked by the occupation of Manila. It accelerated and further promoted the formation of guerrilla groups and other resistance movements.

During that period, people in Badoc were still in their evacuation places. However, they went to town when necessity would arise or anytime they wished to go to do some household chores or visit members of their families.

Bino, like any other male head of a household, had to continue staying in the town as head of a vigilante group to guard their household possessions. There was no government, but there was no anarchy. The vigilantes looked after the security of the whole town. No serious crimes were committed, only a few petty thefts. The vigilantes had to close one eye to those petty incidents, knowing full well that the poor needed some necessities in life. Otherwise, those who had plenty would share what they had with the have-nots. This was the usual recourse, a tradition of the Filipino people, especially at a time of dire necessity.

Disbanded soldiers from the provinces of Ilocos Norte and Ilocos Sur were regrouping to form a guerrilla contingent in Northern Luzon. It was ripe for them to do so, because the Japanese forces at that time had occupied only Laoag, the capital of the province of Ilocos Norte, and Vigan, the capital of Ilocos Sur.

In no time, three groups of guerrilla forces were organized in Ilocos Norte. One group was headed by Major Monje. Inasmuch as his wife was from Bangui, Ilocos Norte, his area of guerrilla activities was from Pagud-pud to other towns in northern part of Ilocos Norte, going south, including Pasuquin, Piddig and Vintar.

The other group was under the command of Captain Madamba. His territory was from Laoag, going south, to cover the towns of San Nicolas, Batac, and Paoay, including the towns east of Laoag, namely Dingras, Bacarra, and Banna. This territory was given to him as his roots were from those places and he knew the terrain like the lines in his palms.

The third group was under the command of Lt. Magno. His guerrilla operations covered the next town, which was Paoay, and went farther south, embracing Currimao, Pinili, Nueva Era, and Badoc, including its outlying areas, encroaching on some areas of the province of Ilocos Sur. Those areas were near the boundaries of the provinces of Ilocos Norte and Ilocos Sur. Incidentally, the lieutenant was from Badoc and the first cousin of Bino.

Disbanded soldiers and officers under General Douglas MacArthur, the newly commissioned commander of the United States Armed Forces of the Far East, otherwise known as the USAFE, rallied behind the local guerrillas of the Ilocos region. Civilians volunteered to be recruited, but the three groups chose not to do so. Either the reservists or the regulars, who took action against the Japanese forces, were inducted into the guerrilla movement. They needed only the best, the experienced, and the disciplined to continue the fight for the cause of the United States and the Philippines. They did not want any casualties-to-be within their outfit.

There were civilian volunteers as cooperators—not as soldiers but as eyes and ears of the guerrilla movement. They were also needed in the movement of goods, supplies, and ammunitions, and, above all, in the production of food items on the farms. Just as the guerrillas needed arms and ammunitions, they needed food to keep them alive and give them the strength to fight.

Jun, as a growing young man, was amazed at the fervor and the love the guerrillas had for their country and their mother country, the United States of America. Sometimes, he entertained those thoughts. He wondered why, after all the hardships they had experienced and the ultimate sacrifice they might offer for their country and the United States at the firing line, did they still wish to undergo the same hardships and probably meet their waterloo?

Answering similar questions within his mind, he said, "They are like us seminarians; we were taught to make sacrifices and even to offer our lives for *"Ad Majorem Dei Gloriam."* In addition, when one is ordained a priest, he has to make a vow of obedience, chastity, and poverty.

More news was heard over the radio. This time, the Japanese Propaganda Corps made a broadcast. "The Japanese Imperial Forces formed the Philippine Executive Commission (PEC) headed by Jorge Vargas on January 23, 1942, in preparation for the institution of a civil government once the whole country is fully occupied."

On the other hand, the clandestine radio reported, "President Roosevelt rejected the Philippine Commonwealth president's proposal of surrender and neutralization."

In defiance of the formation of the PEC and in support of President Roosevelt's rejection of surrender, the guerrillas carefully planned to ambush, at an appropriate time and date, any large Japanese convoy that would snake its way from Laoag to Currimao, a port in Ilocos Norte, to pick up large volume of supplies of food and ammunition for either Laoag or Vigan. Those two provincial capitals were the only seats of the Japanese garrisons in both provinces during that period.

To further demoralize the Filipino people, the Japanese radio sharply blurted out, "Your favorite adopted son, General Douglas MacArthur, has left your country, in defeat, to Australia in February 8. He had abandoned you and put down the Philippines."

In contrast, to buoy up the morale of the people, the clandestine radio in the Philippines announced that General MacArthur had left the Philippines for Australia to regroup the USAFE; but he promised, with his famous words, "I shall return."

Developments in Ilocos Norte during this period, which were deemed appropriate and timely, warranted the implementation of their guerrilla warfare plans. A runner of Lt. Magno contacted Captain Madamba and Major Monje to implement their guerrilla plans.

This runner, Dr. Jose, was a chemist and a professor of a local university in Manila, who was sent to Tokyo before World War II to study at the Tokyo Imperial University. He was able to learn to speak perfect Japanese and write kanji. Everybody thought he was working for the Japanese Imperial Forces, but he was an insider in the guerrilla movement. At the same time, he was an interpreter for the Japanese forces. Being an interpreter, he came to know in advance the plans of the Japanese commanding officer of Ilocos Norte. He even came to know a day in advance when the Japanese rations and ammunitions were to be unloaded at Currimao port, for delivery to Vigan and Laoag. In this regard, he alerted the guerrillas of the day and time when the convoys were to be dispatched to the Japanese garrisons.

It was an early morning of February 15, 1942, immediately after sunrise, when twelve trucks, two vanguard vehicles, and another two trucks at the rear full of Japanese soldiers carried freight from Currimao towards Badoc on their way to Vigan. Between the two vanguard vehicles and the two trucks at the rear were eight trucks. Similarly, all those military vehicles were full of freight, consisting of food supplies and ammunitions. Lt. Magno got all this information from Dr. Jose well in advance. He and his guerrilla force were waiting for their prey. Lt. Magno, as the commanding officer, positioned his company at a cliff, covered by massive tropical trees, overlooking the national highway where the Japanese trucks would roll by.

One company, commanded by his sergeant, placed themselves before the town of Badoc, and another company, under the command of another sergeant, was stationed at the border of Ilocos Norte and Ilocos Sur. The rationale behind the placements of the two companies was to finish any Japanese soldier left alive who might have escaped from the ambush.

Lt. Magno and his company, camouflaged and hiding behind huge boulders at the edge of a cliff, hidden by thick bushes and trees with massive trunks, were ready. Their fingers curled around the triggers of their rifles; their eyes focused on their rifles' sights, aimed at the highway. The soldiers could hear the fast rhythm of their heartbeats. Lt. Magno looked at his watch. He said to himself, "Now is the time. Do or die."

As a devout Catholic, he made the sign of the cross and murmured the Lord's Prayer. Those soldiers who believed in the strength of prayers followed silently. The non-believers simply gave a faint smile. Knowing the habits of their commander, they knew Lt. Magno making the sign of the cross was indicative of the proximity of the enemy; they were minutes away. Hence, they were all prepared to give the opening salvo upon the convoy of Japanese soldiers.

The two trucks acting as vanguards finally appeared at the curve, running at a slow pace, probably about thirty kilometers per hour. Within seconds, a shot rung out. This was followed by the *ra-tat-tat- tat* of machine guns and automatic rifles.

The first truck stopped. The Japanese answered with bursts of their machine guns, followed by rifle pot shots aimed at the cliffs.

The convoy could not immediately turn back. The national highway was a narrow two-lane road. It was not wide enough for the convoy to make a complete U-turn to go back northwards. They had to move fast. As the first truck was engaged in the fight, the second truck tried to accelerate at a high speed, to be followed by the rest of the convoy. Taking advantage of this adverse position of the Japanese, the guerillas, with their trench mortars and hand grenades aimed at the convoy, made direct hits to some of the freight trucks. The burning trucks impeded the advance of the trucks behind them. Hell broke loose. The Japanese soldiers jumped and sought cover within a four-meter-deep irrigation canal. They were at a disadvantaged position because they were at a much lower level than the guerrillas and there were no trenches to shield them.

The Japanese vanguards were completely annihilated. The smell of gun powder permeated the air. Black, thick smoke from the exploding ammunition inside the burning trucks plummeted skywards and could be seen at a distance in the municipality of Badoc.

The Japanese rear guards, however, were able to accelerate and found a space in between the burning freight trucks to go through. The remaining freight trucks followed suit. The guerrilla company, commanded by a sergeant, waited for their targets to come by. The guerrillas were positioned on both sides of the road. On the left side, where there were irrigation ditches used as trenches, were the guerrillas armed with hand grenades and small and short-range guns. Those at the right side at the cliff were armed with heavier arms. As the remaining convoy arrived, at the right time, hand grenades were thrown at the trucks with great precision. The Japanese soldiers jumped out but they were caught by machine gun, automatic, and Springfield rifle shots at the cliff. They were very careful, though, not to hit their comrades at arms on the left side, at a lower level inside the irrigation ditches.

Gunshots, the rapid firing of machine guns and automatic rifles, and the whistling sounds of trench mortar shells arching towards their targets echoed in the town of Badoc and in the nearby barrios.

In a short time, the whole remaining Japanese contingent was completely wiped out. Burning trucks with exploding ammo, and bodies of Japanese soldiers were strewn around the highway. The guerrillas warned the people within the vicinity of the ambush to temporarily evacuate for quite some time. The guerrillas came to learn that where a Japanese soldier was ambushed within a radius of seven kilometers, all people caught within that radius were tortured or executed.

The great ambush in Badoc under Lt. Magno was a great success. The guerrillas had no casualties. On the other hand, the civilians got the brunt. Torture and punishment were meted out upon the civilians by the Japanese forces caught within the vicinity of the ambush. Similar successful ambushes were planned and executed on different days within this period, by Major Monje and Captain Madamba, with their guerrilla units in their respective domains.

Those guerrilla incursions, ambushes, and other activities agitated the Japanese Imperial Forces. The Japanese undertook mopping up operations in the mountains to catch the guerrillas in their dragnets. Japanese scout planes, like eagles with sharp eyes scouring the area for their prey, were busy gliding in the skies.

The guerrillas could not be found. They were like Houdini, who seemingly vanished into thin air. They had bivouacked in other adjacent provinces, namely Apayao and Abra. Gaining access to those provinces was very difficult, especially during the monsoon season, when one had to go through mountain trails, tropical forests, and raging, overflowing rivers.

The Japanese forces had to fortify their garrisons in Laoag and Vigan. They had to maintain and safely run their lines from Currimao port to those two points. They had to safely transport their food and ammunitions to those garrisons.

During those activities, Dr. Jose would inform the guerrillas of the time and day the Japanese would go to Currimao and back to Vigan and Laoag. Relying on the information given, the guerrillas would take pot shots and ambush them at the appropriate time and place, with great success. After such attacks, the guerrillas would seek the safety of the tropical forests. The Japanese, not knowing the terrains of the jungles, were always at a disadvantage.

During that period, guerrilla activities were intensified in other parts of the country. Formation of guerrilla units became widespread throughout the Philippines. The topography and all the physical features of the country, including climate, were conducive to the conduct of guerrilla activities within the seventy-two hundred islands of the Philippines.

In Badoc, a new guerrilla unit was formed by two brothers, known as Lt. Inting and Lt. Pedong. Their unit was loosely formed; hence, it was not a strong unit. However, the unit did some intelligence work and created more problems for the Japanese. Like a small speck of dirt in the eye, it also caused some pains to the Japanese.

Foremost of the guerrilla movements during that period was the *Hukabalahp*. Luis Taruc, its first military commander and head of the movement, formed it on March 29, 1942. At that time, it mainly operated in Tarlac, Pampanga, Bataan, Zambales, and the provinces surrounding Manila. This guerrilla force gained the respect of the Japanese. They were strong in guerrilla warfare and military tactics, and well disciplined. This was in view of their ideology about social reform, which they were fighting for. This made them very united. Both the enemy and the Filipinos eventually recognized them as a strong and cohesive guerrilla force.

Chapter 7

April–June 1942

To contain the guerrilla activities in Ilocos Norte and Ilocos Sur, Japanese garrisons were established in strategic places, aside from those in Laoag and Vigan. One of those was in Badoc.

The Japanese commander of the Badoc Garrison was Captain Ueda. He had about two hundred and fifty men. The municipal hall became their headquarters and the residence of the commander. The elementary school, which was adjacent to the municipal hall, was converted into barracks for the soldiers. The plaza was used as their exercise, military training, and marching ground. It was also the place where town hall meetings and other activities were held.

Cultural shows by the Japanese soldiers, offered to the public for free, were performed at the open auditorium and open theater. These gave the Badoquenos an opportunity to appreciate Japanese culture, especially the Japanese folk music and songs.

In later periods, the place became a notorious venue. People were forcibly assembled there, to be intimidated and terrorized and to witness executions, by musketry or decapitation by a sharp sword, of captured civilians suspected of being guerrillas or sympathizers.

Jun, when he first saw a victim's head roll by, slashed by a sharp sword that could split a human being's hair, was paralyzed with fear. This was not only physically but also had long-term psychological effects.

There was an incident where a woman was suspected of being a cook for the guerrillas. She was brought to the plaza where people were forced to witness. A Japanese military officer stripped her naked. He let her stand on a platform. The Japanese military officer passed a burning bundle of rice straw between her legs, over her genitalia. Her shrieking screams were heard, disturbing the stillness of the silent, frightened crowd. This incident overwhelmed Jun. He would have passed out if it were not for the strength of his mother, Fely, who pulled him upright when he was about to fall forward.

Jun never allowed his inner feelings and body language to expose his real emotions. Giving away his true feelings would enable the Japanese soldiers to identify him as a collaborator of the guerrillas.

The executions and tortures Jun witnessed made him a man overnight. The garrison commander of Badoc, Captain Ueda, and his men never participated in the gruesome executions and punishments of suspected guerrillas. The Japanese Military Police, who were known for their cruelty, did them. The people of Badoc recognized Captain Ueda as a different Japanese officer, who conducted himself with dignity and fairness.

On April 9, 1942, Bataan fell into the hands of the Japanese Imperial Forces under the command of General Masarahu Homma. It was a very sad day for the whole country, especially those whose sons, husbands, and fathers made the ultimate sacrifice for their country and people.

Those who survived Bataan didn't fare any better. Either they were captured or marched to the Japanese concentration camps. Those who were strong and not experiencing any sickness made it to the camp, while the sick and the weak were either bayoneted or shot to death.

Many of those who made the march to the concentration camps were inhumanly incarcerated. Thousands and thousands of them died from malaria, dysentery, and other intestinal diseases. All of them suffered from *avitaminosis* or malnourishment. It was a pitiful sight to behold those in the concentration camps. Both the Americans and Filipinos were physically wasted. Their own skins tightly wrapped their bones, apparently with no muscles.

Adding insult to injury, another lugubrious event occurred. That was the day when President Manuel L. Quezon and Vice President Osmena departed for the United States to set up the Philippine government in exile.

It became more painful and depressing to the Philippines and its people when the Japanese announced over the radio, "The Philippines has finally fallen. General Jonathan Wainwright has surrendered Corregidor, the last bastion of the United States in the Far East. You are now completely abandoned by your so-called leaders, Quezon and Osmena, who flew to the United States."

The faith of the Filipinos in the United States never dwindled. Those negative events further enkindled patriotism, to a point where guerrilla warfare became more intensified. Civilians started to volunteer to join the underground. At this point in time, Bino started to slowly fade away from activities in the town. Day by day, he concealed himself in obscurity, until he had to go elsewhere to hide in the hinterlands.

Bino's family was not able to join him. They had to be left behind. Bino had to be out of sight in public because Mr. Marino, who always accompanied the higher officers of the Japanese Imperial Forces, was looking for him. Mr. Marino advised the Japanese on civilian affairs and public administration. He wanted Bino to become the mayor of Badoc as soon as the civil government in the Philippines was instituted. Incidentally, Mr. Marino was the sponsor in baptism of his daughter, Lea. There was an affinity between them. He was the *compadre* of Bino.

The whole populace of Badoc, even the guerrillas, wanted him to be the future municipal mayor. They honestly believed that he was the right man to lead them and go through the vicissitudes of life, especially at times of adversity and great need. They thought he would be like his father, Capitan Martin.

In the history of Ilocos Norte, Capitan Martin was the last *gubernadorcillo* of the municipality of Badoc during the last years of the Spanish regime, from 1896 to 1898, when the revolutionaries started to have uprisings against Spain. He was widely known as one who had efficiently and diplomatically administered his municipality. He faithfully led his people during those turbulent days of the Spanish-American War. His leadership and administration gave way to a smooth transition from the Spanish to the American regime, by virtue of the Treaty of Paris. He thus continued to be the mayor of Badoc during the first two years of the American regime, from 1898 to 1900. He was always remembered and regarded, even nowadays, as the epitome of local administration.

Bino, on the other hand, was a great contrast to his father. He abhorred politics. During World War I, he was a student of the University of the Philippines, College of Engineering. At that time, the Philippines was a colony of the United States of America. In 1914, together with some of his college friends, he volunteered to join the United States Navy. With America at war, he saw action in the Atlantic Ocean in his ship, the *USS Montana*, from 1914 to 1918.

Immediately after the First World War, he returned to his country. The U.S. government at that time needed American-trained local teachers who successfully finished the American curriculum, which was recognized even by the then Columbia Teachers College. He went to the teacher's training school under an American curriculum at the then Philippine Normal School in Manila. American educators, who were called the Thomasites, trained him. He graduated with honors. He became a mathematics and music teacher and, at the same time, the baseball coach. He was a very qualified mathematics teacher, as records indicated that in the national teachers' civil service examination, he was the only one who got a perfect score in mathematics.

Likewise, his wife Fely was trained to teach English and science after Bino. With Bino's training, background, and attitude, he would be a square peg in a round hole in public administration. He was more of a mentor and a disciplinarian.

Bino continued hiding in an undisclosed place. Only a few guerrillas and trusted relatives and friends knew his daily whereabouts. When Japanese soldiers would go out for their mopping up operations to seek guerrillas and to find him, he would be hiding in a swamp or brook. He would cover himself with water lilies. When need be, he would submerge his head and his whole body under the water, with thick water lilies around to camouflage him and with a reed in his mouth as a snorkel to breathe through.

Sometimes he would be in a very awkward and uncomfortable position for hours. It was incredible how long he endured this situation. After months of hiding, his physical condition deteriorated; but his spirit was never broken. For this reason, he finally came out from his hideaway, returned to his family, and showed his thin and haggard face in public for the first time on June 3, 1942. This was also his youngest child's ninth birthday. This event partly contributed to his making a decision to go out in public. He missed his family.

Chapter 8

July – December 1942

The Japanese Imperial Forces ordered all residents of the municipality of Badoc to go back to town. Those who defied this order were considered sympathizers of the guerrilla movement. People were already aware of the torture and punishment given to guerrilla sympathizers. Without hesitancy, they complied with this directive. Like swarms of white ants coming out from their anthills, they all returned to town from all directions. From the Japanese point of view, the exodus from their evacuation areas was successful.

A day was set for a town meeting. The Japanese expected a very huge assembly. All able-bodied citizens from age thirteen to sixty-five, both male and female, were expected to be there; otherwise, they would be dealt with accordingly.

Under the Japanese rule, *to be dealt with accordingly* meant a sentence given by the military in accordance with the gravity of the offense committed.

Torture, especially water torture, was a part of the punishment. This was one way of forcibly extracting information from suspects about the whereabouts of any guerrilla or hidden arms and ammunitions.

The provincial commander, General Fujita, went to Badoc to preside at the town meeting. His officers and a convoy of about twenty trucks full of soldiers escorted him and gave security to the general.

A handful of well-known politicians, mostly lawyers, accompanied the general. The political color of those politicians was not yet known at that time. Were they pro-Japanese or did they just want to help maintain law and order in the community without necessarily helping the cause of the Japanese Imperial Forces? This was a big question at that time.

At the assembly that was convened by the Japanese in the open auditorium at the town plaza, the commanding officer underscored the Japanese Imperial Forces' plans for immediate implementation.

"Firstly, schools will be opened in the town. A course in the Japanese language will be compulsory. Adults, especially professionals and all the teachers, will take intensive courses in Nippongo." The rationale behind this was to enable them to tutor the younger generation in at-home supplementary courses in Nippongo, in addition to the courses taken in school.

"Secondly, the Japanese will appoint town officials to hold the reigns of civil administration and the former municipal employees, to render local civil service with the close supervision of the Japanese Military Government.

"Thirdly, a complete census must be undertaken. A complete household survey will be done by a group of local civil servants per *barangay* (the smallest unit in society comprised of a number of families living in one designated contiguous area), accompanied by at least a squad of Japanese soldiers, to list the names of the head of households and their dependents, and their respective ages, sex, and addresses.

"The bottom of the form will be signed by the Japanese squad leader, to be pasted at the main door of the house. Individual badges indicating the individual names, ages, sex, and address of each member of the household must be written in Japanese characters, to be signed by the issuing squad leader. Each individual should wear his/her identification badge at all times in front of his shirt or her blouse. The emblem of the rising sun has to be stamped at the top of the badge, to be discernable at a distance by any Japanese soldier. A civilian in the street without such badge as identification shall be dealt with accordingly and be given severe punishment by the Imperial Japanese Forces.

"And fourthly, if a family has a houseguest, it must be immediately reported to the Japanese garrison, indicating his/her name, sex, and address. Similarly, the name must be pasted at the main door of the house, and a badge will be issued, which should be worn in front of his/her shirt or dress for identification. A Japanese soldier together with a Filipino municipal policeman may take an actual head count anytime during the night, at random, in any residential house. On the other hand, if one has to travel and go elsewhere overnight or for a period of time, he/she must report to the garrison. This will take care of the head counts done in the household at night. It is likened to debit and credit in a financial statement. This is to prevent any undesirable elements from hiding in somebody else's house."

Every morning at sunrise, all able-bodied men and women in the town had to assemble in the town plaza. The daily ritual was to bow towards the east when the sun casts its first rays over the mountains. They also bowed towards the east to pay respects to the Japanese emperor. This was equivalent to the flag raising ceremony in the United States and in the Philippines. After the ritual, radio taisho followed. All those morning exercises took more than an hour to accomplish.

Immediately after the morning exercise, the Japanese soldiers in the town plaza would line up, stripped naked, to take their daily morning hot bath, one after the other, in a hot tub. The tub was an empty gasoline barrel full of water. It was on top of three huge flat slabs of stone, formed into a stove, kindled with fire underneath to keep the water warm. The soldiers had no feeling of embarrassment or shame, even if women passed by to go to church. They were like infant toddlers, sans diapers, romping around. The women had no other recourse except to go through the town plaza. They had to place their neckerchiefs over their faces to cover their eyes. This prevented them from seeing a disturbing view of naked soldiers in line for their hot bath.

Jun was enrolled in an intensive Japanese language course, together with the teachers, professionals, municipal officials, and other interested adults. He was then in the same language course with his father, Bino. He was the only non-professional and non-adult in that Nippongo class.

Having taken up Latin in school, he found learning the Nippongo course to be easy. It was a very smooth sailing for him throughout the first semester, as well as in the subsequent intermediate and advanced courses.

In the first semester, he scored highest on the written test. On the oral tests, he was tied with a high school English grammar and English literature teacher. He and the lady schoolteacher had an hour of a Japanese language oral joust. In one of the sentences to be translated into Japanese, she erred. Jun immediately corrected it and won. As a prize, he was given school supplies, canned and dried Japanese food items, medicines, and a box of Akebono, a brand of Japanese cigarettes.

From that time on, the Japanese were very comfortable with Jun, his parents, and the entire family. Captain Ueda would even visit them to play on the piano. Bino, on the other hand, was not comfortable at all. He had to be careful. He was the first cousin of Lt. Magno, the guerrilla commander.

Jun continued to garner first-prize awards in all his Japanese language courses and contests in his hometown. He became popular with Captain Ueda and his soldiers. June concentrated on his Japanese language courses inasmuch as he had nothing to do. It was more or less occupational therapy to assuage the boredom from which he was suffering.

Meanwhile, the Japanese forces continued their mopping up operations to capture any guerrillas on the run. Many of them laid low. There was peace and quiet in Badoc during this period. There were no guerilla activities around the whole municipality and its outlying barrios and areas. It was a peaceful atmosphere.

There were concerts by the local orchestra to entertain the Japanese soldiers and the public every Sunday afternoon. Some guerrillas, who were incognito, were amongst the public, attending and enjoying the concerts.

Jun played the baritone horn in the orchestra. This gave him the opportunity to learn and play overtures and classical music, such as by Rossini, Bach, Beethoven, and Mozart.

On certain occasions, there were folk dances, including Japanese numbers, *kabuki* style, performed by Japanese soldiers. Captain Ueda, who loved cultural shows and ballroom dancing, would invite local socialites, politicians, teachers, and other professionals for a dance party, with the local orchestra playing. At those parties, Jun displayed his talents in ballroom dancing. He learned the tango, rhumba, waltz, and other ballroom dances from his sister, Ariana.

On special occasions, General Furuki and the provincial officials were invited to attend such events. The atmosphere during those functions was more of a fiesta. There was pomp and splendor.

On October 14, 1942, the president of the Civil Government of the Republic of the Philippines, the Honorable Jose P. Laurel, was inaugurated. He was formerly the chief justice of the Supreme Court of the then Commonwealth of the Philippines. With the civil government installed, the guerrillas laid low. Life in the rural areas seemed to have returned to normal. Farmers tilled their lands and brought their farm goods to town for sale on market days. School children went back to school. Lifestyles went back to how they were before the occupation. Only certain luxury and imported necessary items could not be found in the market. There seemed to be a feeling of peace during this period.

Chapter 9

First Half of 1943

As noted earlier, the civil government of the Philippines was already instituted. The Japanese forces made an announcement, in conjunction with the civil government's establishment, that amnesty would be given to all guerrillas who would immediately lay down their arms. They would be sent to rehabilitation centers, as opposed to concentration camps, where they would undergo physical rehabilitation and treatment, combined with educational and political indoctrination.

Guerrillas who were sick took advantage of this amnesty. Similarly, those who were already used to the safety and warmth of their own homes took the benefits of this offer.

More secondary schools and colleges opened their doors to eager students. Trade took place between provinces. Agricultural production rose tremendously as compared to the previous periods.

Competitive sports, such as baseball, basketball, tennis, boxing, wrestling, etc., between schools, colleges, and provinces spread like wildfire.

Normalcy occurred in the public and private sectors. Night clubs with floor shows glittered with neon and colored lights, and stage shows and vaudevilles flourished. Local alcoholic beverages, such as San Miguel

Beer, Tan-duay rum, and wines made from various local fruits and berries overflowed in bars. Concerts by the symphony orchestra; ballet companies; the local sopranos, tenors, and baritones; and stage shows had their grand nights. Everything seemed normal.

Trucks, cars, and trains ran between cities, towns, and provinces. Due to lack of gasoline, they had to depend on local alternative sources of energy. There was abundance of charcoal from trees and coconut shells and husks to use as alternative sources of energy. Different forms of transportation were extensively used, from railways to horse drawn *calesas*, bull carts, sledges, and of course the old reliable bicycles. There were rafts and boats in the waterways.

Food processing, textile, and light engineering industries emerged. They manufactured products to meet local demands by utilizing local materials, showing the ingenuity of the Filipino people even during wartime. It was incredible. There was progress.

Jun had to visit his family's farms in different barrios. He rode on horseback like an American cowboy, with a wide-brimmed hat to protect him from the scorching tropical sun as he trotted towards their farms. He always looked forward to supervising the harvesting of rice and other farm produce.

Their tenants welcomed his presence because he was a polite and nice guest. Jun, likewise, enjoyed every minute he was in the rural areas, because their tenants were hosts with the most. They would roast a suckling pig, locally known as *lechon*, which was served to the harvesters. Jun loved gourmet food. They always served him this food. They knew that he always savored lechon with gusto. Being the son of the landowner, he was given this honor of being served first and tasting the *lechon* before others, as was the usual custom in rural areas in the Philippines,

Jun would relish the crispy skin of the roasted pig, with fat adhered to the skin. It was dipped in the homemade salsa made out of the pig's liver. He usually took the crispy skin with a chaser, a local alcoholic beverage fermented from the sugar cane juice, known as *basi*. It had the color and taste of English sherry. After downing two to three glasses of basi, he would feel the warmth of his blood rushing into his cheeks. He loved this sensation. He was not yet sixteen. He was not supposed to touch alcoholic beverages yet; but it was wartime. Life was uncertain and so short. Society gave him dispensation. They said, "Let him experience it." He would then doze off under the shade of a tree, inebriated by the basi and the balmy breeze caressing his face.

In April, the town fiesta was held. Different barrios participated. Dances, musical programs, and other wholesome frivolities were held. People indulged in parties with sumptuous food. Similarly, the Japanese soldiers became more complacent, as they saw people indulging in the pleasures of life.

The tranquility, the enjoyment, and all the pleasurable activities were more of an opiate to the townspeople. It seemed there was no war. There was a seeming compatibility between the citizens of Badoc and the Japanese forces during that period. That was one reason why the Japanese forces were good to the people of Badoc.

Captain Ueda became an institution. He was respected. Unwittingly, on some occasions, he used to dine in parties with guerrillas, who remained incognito and inactive. The civilians, the guerrillas, and the Japanese soldiers took advantage of the air of peace permeating the community.

Like a jigsaw puzzle where all pieces fall in their proper places, the right environment and ingredients enabled both sides to have peace. That could have been the lull before the storm.

Deep within the hearts of the people, they prayed for the return of the Americans. They longed for the freedom of speech and of the press, freedom to choose public officials. All of these were denied. They missed those freedoms, which were given freely by the Americans during their regime.

The social events during that period stirred positive action on the part of the Japanese forces. Captain Ueda, characterized by social graces, requested that the mayor of Badoc, Mayor Nito, invite the town's crème of society for dinner and dancing. He was to give a farewell party. He was being promoted to a higher post in Laoag, where he was going to work directly under General Furuki.

Incidentally, Captain Ueda, presumably a bachelor, had an eye on a Philippine socialite and a resident of Badoc. She was a well-known student leader during her college days and, at the same time, a socialite in Manila. She was called Vel, smart and charming, proportionately endowed with the right form in the proper places. She was a good dancer and, above all, had social graces. She had the "it" factor. She was a lady all men would wish to have and to hold as a partner for life.

Captain Ueda, having known Jun because of his expertise in Nippongo and having visited his house from time to time to play on the piano, invited him, as well as his sisters and parents, to the party. Nearly all the prominent people of Badoc were invited to that social event.

Three classrooms of the school were converted into a dance hall. It was easy to transform them into one big hall, as the walls were knockdowns. Local officials did not have a hand in the decorating. The Japanese soldiers did.

The people looked forward to attending or witnessing the ball. It had been a long time since a dinner-dance was held for the crème of society in Badoc.

The heavily guarded gate opened for the much-awaited big night. The Japanese officers and their entourage arrived. In full regalia, they gave an air of superiority and authority to the hall.

Captain Ueda, the host, together with his commanding officer, General Furuki, and their military aides, were at the door receiving the guests. They followed the Japanese protocol. They graciously bowed to each guest as he or she entered the dance hall. The way they carried themselves emitted respect and honor, which were bestowed automatically by the public.

Upon crossing the dance floor and being ushered to their rightful place, guests explored the hall with their eyes and were amazed. They said to each other, "What a beautiful sight! The decorations are so simple but unique and elegant." Guests were overwhelmed by the set up of the dance hall.

Outside, beside the building, Japanese lanterns were hung under the branches of acacia trees. They swung each time there was a gust of wind. When seen at a distance in the darkness of the night, they seemed like fireflies glowing and sparkling in the wilderness.

In the ballroom, strips of crepe paper of different colors were meticulously strung and strewn in the appropriate places. Cut out geometric figures made from pieces of colored drawing papers were hung and fastened to the ceiling with a string, alternating with origami art pieces done by hand by the Japanese soldiers. The artistic nature of the Japanese was reflected in the hall. There was color and harmony intrinsic to the Japanese culture.

As the guests settled down in their assigned seats, the live band began to play, together with the public singing. *"Mi-yo to-o-ka-i no, su-ra-ake-te ..."* This song was compulsory, learned by all citizens, to be sung as the Japanese Imperial Forces anthem. This was followed by the Philippine national anthem, at that time, "Lupang Mapalad." The lyrics were set appropriately for the Japanese regime by the civil government. The melody, however, was the music of the old traditional Philippine national anthem, "Land of the Morning."

The orchestra opened the dance floor with the waltz, the strains of Strauss. Captain Ueda, General Furuki, their military aides, and the provincial and municipal officials, with their dance partners, glided, waltzed, and opened the dance floor. Mayor Nito handpicked the dance partners of the Japanese officers. They were selected based on their social graces, ballroom dance proficiency, and education. Of course, Vel, the apple of the eye of Captain Ueda, was the captain's partner. It seemed that the Japanese officers diligently did their homework. They gracefully danced with intricate waltz steps, which only an experienced ballroom dancer would dare to publicly exhibit. The Japanese soldiers rendered some floor shows, musical numbers, and skits a la kabuki, to the amusement of the local guests.

The orchestra played various musical pieces, not only the waltzes but also the jazz music of Benny Goodman, Glen Miller, Louis Armstrong, and Harry James, and the Latin Beat of Xavier Cugat, etc. The orchestra was versatile and dynamic.

After the opening dance, the orchestra played another tune, "Girl of My Dreams." As the first note was played, Jun stood and looked around to select a dance partner. His eyes wandered, seeking one. In doing so, his eyes met the eyes of a young, smart-looking, and charming girl his age. She was Chita.

There was something in that first encounter. That eye contact was meaningful as if they already understood each other. He approached her, bowed slightly, and offered his hand for a dance. She stood and gracefully made a curtsy. This was the protocol at that time when a gentleman would request a lady for a dance. Immediately, Jun placed his right hand on her back, slightly above her waistline, with his left hand clasping her right hand, and swept her to the dance floor to the tune of "Girl of My Dreams " He sung softly into her ears with the melody being played while they were dancing. Jun whispered to her, "I mean everything the song wished to convey." As Jun looked into her eyes, she looked up at him with her lips slightly opened, as if ready to receive a warm kiss, like a rose bud about to open readily to catch the dew drops in the early morning. Instinctively, he pressed his lips onto hers, imprinting his love for her.

At that moment, his parents were also dancing to the same tune. As they swirled and turned, their eyes caught Jun planting a kiss on Chita's lips. Bino then saw a picture of himself as a young man in Jun, and likewise, Fely, in the person of Chita. That incident brought Bino and Fely back to yesteryears. They reminisced about those momentous events in their youth.

Bino told Fely, "Looking at your son, do you remember our first dance?"

Fely replied, "Yes I do. See how time flies. It seems like yesterday."

Both felt they were young again. Energized by those memories, they continued turning, swaying, and swirling to the tune of the three-fourth beat. They even remembered the golden voiced Rudy Valee, who sang "Girl of My Dreams," the very melody they were dancing to.

As they were dancing, Jun softly conveyed to Chita, "How I wish the hands of time would stand still. I want to hold you in my arms forever."

Chita heard him but remained silent. However, she pressed her body close to Jun. Jun felt her heaving bosom. She turned her face up with endearing eyes. Jun understood then what her body language conveyed. But the night had to end. It was an event to remember always.

When the entire family went home, Bino and Fely approached Jun. They did not tell him what they observed on the dance floor. But they asked him, "After the war, will you go back to the seminary?"

Jun replied, "Time will tell."

Every day, without missing a day, Jun was at Chita's house. They loved to do things together, especially playing with duets on the piano.

They made plans for the future. They used to tell each other, "After the war, let us go back to school, and then to college."

They did not know what professions they would pursue. They were not yet focused, because during wartime, they had to live on a day-to-day basis. However, they entertained in their minds. "After college, the church bells will ring so merrily; and we shall march down the aisle. We shall raise a big family and live happily thereafter." Their affair was not puppy love. They were really deeply in love.

Jun's parents were sure then that he would never go back to the seminary. Bino told his wife, "I am definitely sure your son will not become a priest. He will never go back to the seminary. In the first place, he should have not behaved the way he did on the dance floor. He was publicly displaying a sign of affection with that beautiful young girl. Furthermore, he loves dancing."

Fely responded, with regret in her voice, "I wanted him to be a minister of God, to be a Jesuit. He lost his vocation; but he found his new love."

Chapter 10

Second Half of 1943

Guerrillas in Ilocos Norte who took advantage of the amnesty were sent to the Rehabilitation and Indoctrination Center in Bongabong, Nueva Ecija. This center was more than four hundred kilometers southeast of the Ilocos region. They were encamped in that center for more than six months.

After their indoctrination, they were sent back to their respective homes. They were obligated to report twice or thrice a week to the Japanese garrison in their respective hometowns. For this reason, they were not yet ready to regroup and go to their respective bivouac to prepare for their next phase of guerrilla activities and warfare.

Taking advantage of that situation, the guerrillas from Ilocos Sur, which was another faction, crossed the border of Ilocos Norte and started to entrench themselves and gain a foothold in Badoc. Captain Dionie headed this group.

In the meantime, the replacement for Captain Ueda arrived. He was Captain Magota. He was tall for a Japanese man. He was burly and had a gait that created a feeling of antipathy and fear. He came with his own men. A new batch of Japanese soldiers occupied the garrison; thus, all new faces of Japanese soldiers were seen in the town.

He must have had some forethought that guerrillas were preparing for an offensive. He let the garrison be more fortified. More pillboxes were built for machine gunners and automatic riflemen. More trenches were dug. Barbed wires were strewn along the coiled wire fences already surrounding the garrison, which became a double protection.

One early morning in October 1943, the guerrillas, under Captain Dionie, raided the poblacion of Badoc. They fired the first salvo. It was about 2:30 a.m. Rifle shots and the rapid-fire shots of automatic rifles and machine guns were heard near the Japanese garrison.

The Japanese answered back with trench mortar fires. Bino knew that those loud and deep booming sounds, which seemed to make eardrums burst, were those of trench mortars. When a trench mortar shell was fired, there was the first bang. Then, it was followed by a whistling and petrifying sound, arching its way to its target; and finally, a very loud explosion would be heard once it hit its target or the ground.

The guerrillas set fire to houses taken at random. Why they did this, the populace did not know.

While the raid was going on, Bino called all members of his family, one by one, in the living room. Once assembled, he ordered them, "Go downstairs through the trap door in the dining room for safety. Stay in a prone position and stay away from the windows."

They complied with the command, and one by one, they went down through the narrow trap door. The ground floor was cement with thick walls, like any antique Spanish house in the Philippines. It was about two feet thick, made out of bricks and joined by cement.

All of them were all in a prone position and sought cover behind those thick walls and avoided places near windows.

Poor Jun was all shook up again. Houses surrounding their residence were razed to the ground by fire. The whole town of Badoc was an inferno. Tongues of fire played and leaped from one rooftop to the other. Many houses had thatch roofs and split bamboo walls, which were flammable.

Inside Bino's house, the heat became more intense as other neighboring houses were on fire. Jun was terrified. He told his dad, "I am afraid our house may catch fire. I can feel the searing heat. We might be scorched or singed inside the house."

Bino took Jun's statement seriously. He had the same fears. Either the guerrillas intentionally spared Bino's house in view of the thick walls in which they also sought cover, or a strong gush of wind might have swayed the direction of the fire, preventing the house from being gutted.

Bino thought the situation would get worse. He signaled his whole family to follow him northwards and told them, "Let us go and evacuate to barrio Parang."

Without any delay, each gathered his or her few necessary personal belongings, such as mosquito nets, blankets, and some personal effects. Hurriedly, all of them sprinted out from the house. They ran and then sought cover as the trench mortar shells whistled over their heads. The conflagration and tracer bullets flashing inches above their heads illuminated their way towards the fringe of the town. Beyond that was pitch darkness.

Bino instructed his family, "Look out the corner of your eyes in order to have vision in the dark."

For hours and hours, under cover of darkness, they traversed rice fields, which were muddy. To go through a muddy field even for a short distance would sap one's energy and would take many hours. They braved the malaria mosquitoes buzzing over their heads, with arms flailing to drive away the insects that stung their exposed faces and limbs.

As darkness of the night faded and the first rays of the sun were about to penetrate the thick bushes and branches of trees, Bino spotted the trail going towards the direction of Barrio Parang. The trail was very narrow. It allowed only three persons abreast to get through. It was winding, following the banks of the Badoc River. Both sides were lined up with tall eucalyptus trees, old trees with massive trunks, bushes, and underbrush. Trees spread out their branches, which canopied the trail from above.

Bino and his family had to cross the waist-deep river in order to avoid crossing the national highway. This way, they could elude any encounters with Japanese soldiers who might use the national highway from Laoag to give assistance to the Japanese in Badoc.

Bino crossed first, and with a hand signal, he indicated that all was clear. The rest of the family followed suit and crossed the river one by one at intervals of ten minutes. Since they were eight in all—including Jun's cousin, who was a medical doctor, and Concha, their helper—it took them about one hour and twenty minutes to be at the other side of the river. They had to do this to prevent anyone being caught by the Japanese soldiers who might be near there.

Where they crossed, there was no place to hide. There were no trees except and only open space. This was one of the most harrowing moments of Jun's life. If caught by the Japanese, one's head would roll.

After they had crossed the river, Bino asked everybody, "Have you seen the rest of the trail?"

They looked around until frustration hit them because they could not find any trace of it.

Bino's face lit up with an idea. He studied the formation of the eucalyptus trees, the shrubs, and the foliage that might have covered the trail. Bino, while pointing where it might be in the direction where the trees and underbrush were lined up, requested Jun, "Go there and find the trail."

Jun went as instructed, and with great excitement, he yelled, "Dad, that is the trail. Run! The trail is here."

Everybody did. Once they reached the trail, they knew they were already safe. The trail was lined up with trees, *karimboaya* (a variety of cactus), and bushes so thick they veiled the view of anybody several meters away. That gave them a feeling of better security.

Their determination to reach Parang safely led them to walk faster. To ease his tired legs and aching feet, Jun silently sang a song, walking in cadence with the beat and melody of a march in his mind, "The Battle Hymn of the Republic."

About one thousand yards away, Bino saw houses lined up and clustered on terraces beside a mountain. He pointed at them and told his family, "That is our evacuation place, Parang. Once we arrive there, we shall look for the house of Rosalia."

Rosalia was a public school teacher in Pinili Ilocos Norte. When she was a high school student in Badoc, she stayed in Bino's house like a member of the family. That was why Bino and his family felt free to seek her.

A farmer riding at the back of a carabao, with a hand plow strung over his shoulder like a rifle, was coming from the opposite direction. Since the trail was narrow, the whole family stopped and stepped aside to give way to the carabao with the farmer astride. Bino asked the farmer. "Would you kindly direct us to the house of Maestra Rosalia?"

The farmer replied, "With great pleasure. You follow me, and I shall direct you."

Within a short time, they were at the gate of Rosalia's house. In those days, houses in the Philippines had no doorbells. To indicate that somebody outside wanted to get into the house without knocking at the door, one would simply say, "Apo-o-o!" in a polite and modulated voice. This was the local custom in the Ilocos region. Bino did this.

Somebody stirred inside the house. The movement was audible. Lucia, the auntie of Rosalia, heard the salutation. She appeared at the door. To her great astonishment, she saw Bino and the entire family.

With open arms and an open heart, she told them, "Please come up; have a rest first before you have your lunch. In the meantime, have some snacks. I am sure you are all tired and hungry. I am very happy you thought of us, as evidenced by your coming here. We are greatly privileged to have you. Stay here as your evacuation place as long as you wish. You have some farms in this barrio, and your produce will be enough to feed you all. Please make yourself at home, although we do not have the same amenities as you have in your place."

Rosalia, still clad in her nightgown, hurriedly changed into a more appropriate dress to meet the guests. She came out from her bedroom and, much to her surprise, she saw the whole family with whom she had stayed for four years when she was a student in Badoc. She hugged all their guests, one by one. There was a reunion amongst them. They set back the hands of time and remembered those happy days when she was in high school and temporarily became a part of Bino's household .

The following day the capitan del barrio (head of the village) ran through the barrio's main street. He shouted and warned everybody, "Run for your lives. The Japanese are coming this way. Go to your hiding places as fast as possible."

Everybody did. Rufino, Rosalia's father, led Bino and the rest of the family into a cavern good for twelve people. It was situated on a side of the mountain, with its side sliding down towards the base of another slope of a hill, which was the entrance. It was covered with dried and fresh grasses, which appeared to be natural vegetation inherent to the place. Where the slope was were old trees, with huge barks and branches spread out widely and the less matured branches shooting majestically upwards. Thick bushes were abundant at the mouth of the entrance.

Even at the covered entrance, one would not notice the existence of a hideaway. It was pitch dark inside except for some illumination from the rays of light that penetrated in between the spaces of leaves, branches, grasses, and bushes that covered the entrance. Rufino stayed with Bino and the rest of the family, as he no longer had time to rush out and go with his own family.

After a little while, they heard the barking of dogs at a distance. They bent their ears more keenly. Heavy footsteps were heard. They came nearer and nearer to the cavern. Perhaps a squad of Japanese soldiers went their way, several feet from the entrance of the cavern. The whole family heard the voices of the Japanese outside. Their footsteps became louder and louder as they moved to and fro in front of the cavern. The footsteps of the Japanese were very audible, even at a distance, because a horseshoe-shaped piece of metal was nailed to the soles of their shoes. This was to prevent the soles from wearing down quickly.

Everybody in the cavern was nervous, speechless, and breathless. One could hear the rustle of the leaves and cracking of dried twigs stepped upon by the soldiers outside. Jun was filled with fear and badly shaken. Amongst them, he was the most frightened. At this moment, seconds seemed an eternity. No one moved. There was complete silence. All eyes were centered on the entrance, expecting Japanese soldiers, with fixed bayonets at the tips of their rifles, to make the final thrust into their bodies.

Unexpectedly, steps perceived by the ear were going farther and farther away. The barking of dogs was heard at a distance. Everybody gave a sigh of relief. Indications were that the Japanese soldiers had returned to town.

The evacuees still stayed in the cavern until someone close to them and trusted by Rufino came and said, "All is clear."

Jun fervently made the sign of the cross and said, "Deo Gratias." As fast as the wind, everybody exited from the cavern."

As days went by in Parang, there was boredom on the part of the evacuees. Jun became restless; he did not know what to do. He had already read all the old magazines, novels, and other reading materials within his reach. Finally, a thought came into his mind, *How shall I break the monotony of life in this place? I cannot simply go out and fish in the river or take my slingshot and hunt for game birds. The Japanese might just pop in for mopping up operations without any warning from the guerrilla runners; and I might be a victim of Japanese entrapment, only to be tortured in the garrison.* He kept on entertaining this thought and at the same time breaking his head thinking of what he should do.

Like an electric bulb that suddenly lit up, a bright idea came into his mind. He thought of his harmonica and ocarina. He fished them out from his laundry bag wherein he dumped all his personal belongings.

He played first on his ocarina to the delight of his parents. The melody that was played was "Deep Purple." It was like perfume that wafted its scent in the desert air or like a yacht on a windless day, drifting on a calm sea. Everybody who heard him play urged him, "Bravo! Encore! Play some more!"

He complied and played more tunes until he became a victim of the Law of Diminishing Returns and boredom set in again.

They had not heard the drone of airplanes for quite some time. They could not believe it. There was a scout plane hovering above. Papers were thrown from the airplane like snowflakes dropping slowly to the ground. Jun ran out of the house and retrieved the leaflets. In it was a *Noticia*. "All evacuees should return to town immediately. Anybody caught outside shall be dealt with accordingly."

Jun handed the notice to his father. Bino fully understood what the Japanese meant by "shall be dealt with accordingly."

It was obvious what he should do. He called all the members of his family and told them, "It is imperative that we go back to town as soon as possible." He showed them the notice. They welcomed the notice inasmuch as they were already bored and tired of playing the dangerous game of hide-and-seek with the Japanese.

They immediately told their hosts that they should proceed to town as soon as possible. Lucia, Rosalia, and Rufino understood the situation of Bino and his family. Although agreeing with Bino's decision, their hosts wish they could stay in Parang until the war ended.

Rufino took out his two-wheeled cart that was long kept at the barn. The wheels had no tires. They were made out of wood, including the spokes. The cart's chassis had an inverted trapezoid shape, made out of bamboo. It had two bamboo poles attached to the cart, and at the end was the yoke. In between those poles was the cow, with the yoke set on its neck. The cow started pulling the cart, which was fully loaded. There were twelve passengers, including the one who held the reins; hence, it moved so slowly it felt as if time stood still. Anyway, after more than two hours, they finally arrived in the town.

Chapter 11

January to July 1944

There was plenty of tidying up needed in Bino's residence, especially surrounding the house. In inspecting the house, Jun saw that the brick and concrete walls bore telltale marks of bullet holes.

The first thing Fely did was to go to her garden. Upon opening the garden gate, she gave a loud moan and cried, "Oh my, oh my! My garden is in shambles; everything is destroyed!"

Foliage, shrubs, and flowering plants were all dried up. A lot of things had to be replaced. Fely was completely devastated, as many of her favorite flowering plants, especially the jasmine, the gardenias, and the roses, were all dried up. Fely had to wait for at least another four to five months for the rainy season to arrive before her plants were replaced.

Several weeks after arriving in town, there were some developments. Mayor Nito was going to be replaced by Dr. Gus. Dr. Gus had just come back from the rehabilitation center in Bongabong, Neuva Ecija. The Japanese wanted to place him as the mayor of Badoc to show the people of Ilocos Norte a guerrilla sympathizer who was rehabilitated and could be trusted by them.

The guerrillas were most happy, too, to see those new developments. They knew that Dr. Gus was and always would be on their side. It would be to their great advantage.

The time came. Dr. Gus was inducted and sworn in as mayor in early March of 1944. On that day, two men went to the home of Bino, accompanied by his relative. They made sure that no one saw or followed them. As they entered the house, Jun saw that the two men whispered something into his father's ears. What they told Bino was they were in the guerrilla movement. They needed Jun's assistance because of his expertise in Nippongo.

They had already requested Mayor Gus to recommend Jun to be an orderly of Captain Magota and at the same time act as an Ilocano/Japanese interpreter. The die was cast. Since the Japanese forces already had their official English/Japanese interpreter, Jun was appointed as the Ilocano/Japanese interpreter. The Japanese never suspected Jun was working with the guerrillas because of his age. He, therefore, became handy to the guerrilla movement as their eyes and ears on the movements of the Japanese.

The two men spoke to Jun secretly in his bedroom. Even Bino was not present when they were giving instructions to Jun and explaining to him his terms of reference and duties. To motivate and inspire Jun, they told him, "Despite your age, you are doing a great task for our country. All of us, especially your dad, will be very proud of you. Because of your knowledge of Nippongo, you will have access to much information, which you will secretly convey to us. That information will be very important to the underground. You will greatly facilitate the U.S. Armed Forces in the Pacific to defeat the Japanese Imperial forces."

Jun was elated. He was very proud that he was given an opportunity to do a man's job, especially for his country. Jun replied to the two guerrillas, "I shall perform my duties to the utmost of my ability, for the love and greater glory of my country and the United States of America, our mother country."

The two guerrillas further assured Jun, "Don't be scared. The Japanese will never suspect you that you are aiding the underground. They will not suspect a boy of your age of performing a very important secret assignment."

Foremost of Jun's duties was to relay messages, through a runner, about any impending mopping up operation the Japanese in Badoc would undertake. What Jun was supposed to do was to first discern whether the Japanese forces would be undertaking any mopping up operations. He would know when soldiers would prepare their knapsacks, clean their rifles, and prepare their combat shoes and leggings, and when the commander would then brief them on their strategy.

Once Jun had determined that the Japanese were going for their mopping up operations at night, when darkness would set in, he would light a candle or an oil lamp and place it on his window sill. Jun's bedroom was located at the southeast corner of their house. The bedroom had two adjoining windows, one in the east and the other in the south. Jun would place the light on the windowsill in the east. The runner who would be on guard duty would see that light. He was inconspicuously located in a nipa hut almost at the top of a hill overlooking Jun's room. Incidentally, that hill, planted with bamboo trees and fruit trees, belonged to Bino. It was about a kilometer away from Jun's house.

Once the runner saw the light on the window sill, he would get his hallow bamboo tube, about two feet long, and beat it twice, producing a mellow resounding sound, with an interval of about ten seconds of complete silence. He would beat it again with the same interval, repeating it several times with a hammer made out of sun-dried bamboo. The sound emitted was a deep "Boom. Boom," followed by silence for ten seconds, to be repeated as many times as possible until the other runner relayed the same message to the next runner, and so on, until it reached the last runner. He would monitor and verbally relay the message to the guerrillas, telling them that the Japanese were preparing for mopping up operations. The runners were secretly situated and distanced about four hundred meters apart from each other, up to the guerrilla's headquarters.

In the morning, when the first rays of the sun would greet the coming of another day through Jun's bedroom windows, Jun would give a signal if the Japanese were going out for mopping up operations. He would get a mirror, rest it on the windowsill, place it against the sun, and focus the reflection towards the hut at the top of the hill. Otherwise, if it was overcast and he could not reflect any sunlight, he would simply draw a white curtain that hung over the window. The first runner on the hill would similarly relay the message by conking the bamboo tube, which was their usual signal. Subsequent runners would do the same until the message reached the guerrilla's headquarters. Experience indicated that this was the fastest, most secure, and the most reliable way of sending codified messages to the guerrilla headquarters.

The Japanese were assembling at the Badoc plaza in preparation for their mopping up operations. That was the day that tried Jun's spirit, his first test on the job.

As soon as Jun knew that the Japanese were going out, he immediately ran into his bedroom. As the sunlight in the early morning was just peeping over the ranges of the Cordillera Mountains in Ilocos and its first rays were penetrating through cumulus clouds, Jun readily took out a four-inch-by-two-inch face mirror, which he always kept under his pillow, with trembling hands. He was so nervous and had to collect his nerves. He set the mirror against the sunlight and *presto*, the reflected light found its target—the hut at the top of the hill. The message was very timely.

The runners had already relayed the message by conking their bamboo tubes. The guerrilla headquarters received the message as fast as the wind carried the deep and resonant sounds through fields, creeks, and mountains. The guerrillas had plenty of time to move to the adjoining provinces, which were mountainous and thick with tropical forests.

In the meantime, the guerrillas from Ilocos Sur invited the guerrillas headed by Monje, Madamba, and Magno, all USAFE veterans from Ilocos Norte, to regroup themselves and join them in a designated bivouac. Since Captain Dionie was a comrade-in-arms, the three guerrilla groups accepted the invitation. While the Japanese were mopping up in the forests of Badoc, the guerrillas regrouped and went to Abra province, the designated bivouac.

The Japanese found not a single guerrilla. They became belligerent and took able-bodied male civilians from eighteen to fifty-five years of age. They were able to catch in a dragnet those who were not able to hide. They brought them to the Badoc garrison and interrogated them. The town mayor asked Jun to interpret for the captured civilians.

Captain Magota acceded to the wish of the mayor for an Ilocano/Japanese interpreter. Jun was summoned to the garrison. He saw about nine men, all hanging by a rope with their hands tied behind their backs. Their toes were barely touching the floor, giving them an adverse psychological effect, which made them so frustrated that they prayed for death to end the agony they were already suffering. Their feet were centimeters away from the floor, so close to taking a foothold and having a rest, but they could not reach. This further aggravated their suffering.

Jun advised them in Ilocano, which was not at all understood by the Japanese, not to give any positive reply, no matter what. Jun emphasized those words: "No matter what." Jun sternly told them, "If you admit that you are sympathizers of the underground movement or divulge any knowledge of their whereabouts and places where they hide their arms and ammunitions, you will surely jeopardize the safety and lives of civilians, including your families in your barrios, and above all, your own lives. Keep your lips sealed and never reveal any truth. Remember, once you admit that you belong to the underground, you have already dug your own graves. I will never be able to help you."

Jun saw mixed feelings in their eyes; they were begging for mercy, had a look of terror, were feeling intense pain, or simply had a look of resignation. Jun was also shook up, his teeth gritting with nervousness. He was so scared but tried to maintain his composure so as not to betray what was cooking within him.

A short but heavily set Japanese military officer, with his right hand holding his sword encased in its scabbard, suddenly appeared at the interrogation hall.

A very bright electric light was focused, rotating from one end to the other, on the nine men, all in a linear position, hanging from a huge manila rope. The bright rotating light might have had a nauseating effect on the captives. The captain started to interrogate each of them. Jun was silently praying hard that no one would succumb to the torture and reveal the truth.

The Japanese captain ordered one soldier to bring down one captive. He commanded the soldier to let the man lay down, face upward. The man obeyed while the other eight witnessed. The soldier placed a rubber hose, the circumference of which was as large as his arms, into the man's mouth. With a water hose, he poured a pail full of water, with rice bran, into the captive's mouth until the stomach of the man bulged like a pot bellied pig.

The rice bran in the water irritated the captive's throat with scratchy sensation, which made the man cough with pain. The captain questioned the man, and Jun interpreted it in Ilocano. First, Jun told him, "Remember what I told you." Then he continued interpreting what the captain was shouting at the man in a very loud voice. "Are you a guerrillero? Do you know where your companions are? Do you know of any arms or ammunitions hidden somewhere else?"

The man gave a negative reply.

Right away, the Japanese captain ordered the soldier to give the man the water torture again. The soldier went up and stood on the table. Using the table like a diving board above a swimming pool, the soldier, with his heavy boots on, jumped on the bulging stomach full of water until water came out from the man's nose, mouth, and probably all his body cavities.

The man passed out, but the Japanese soldier revived him. One after the other, all the nine men were interrogated and given the same water torture. Jun tried hard to maintain composure without flinching, until one man gave up, telling them that he was a bolo man.

Jun felt he was betrayed; his knees were about to buckle. He was able to hold the edge of a table and propped himself up.

The Japanese captain summoned the town mayor and ordered that all people in town should assemble in the town plaza to witness the execution of the bolo man.

The following morning, the townspeople assembled in the town plaza. The final hour came. The man was led out from the garrison with his eyes blindfolded with a black cloth. His hands were tied behind his back with a manila rope. His shoulders slumped forward and downwards; and with slow measured steps, he walked, dragging his feet, as he was led towards the execution platform. The man was asked to kneel to say his last prayers. He did. He was told to raise his head upright. The officer, with his sword drawn from the scabbard, raised his arm and swiftly swished the sword and sharply cut his neck. With the head decapitated, the body jerked upwards and then rolled to the ground, followed by a fountain of blood spurting from where the head came off.

The execution was a very ghastly scene. People could not help but throw up. Jun was petrified. He could not move from his place until the mayor went to him and extricated him from where he stood. After that, Bino took Jun and shook him back to consciousness; but he remained speechless with his eyes wide open, staring blankly at nothing. It took days before he could act normal. He would sweat profusely in his sleep and shout in his sleep, and had nightmares since then. He had a terrible, traumatic experience. He needed help, but there was no professional help nearby. Only his father, with only minimal training in educational psychology in college and practical experience in school as a teacher, could give Jun guidance through the duration of the war.

The experience Bino and his family had on that execution day made him come up with a great resolution. He finally decided that they had to evacuate again—this time for good and to a farther and deeper place in the mountains abundant with thicker forests and foliage.

The decision was postponed. Bino had a stroke, which paralyzed half of his body. Jun and his mother Fely and the rest of the family were devastated. They thought that was the end of the rope of their lives. Their greatest support in the family was stricken down. Jun told his mother, "I am now a grown up man, no longer a boy. I shall step up and take the place of Daddy."

Fely, with tears in her eyes, replied, "With the experience and all the incidents that have beset your path, I now have the greatest faith in you, with Gold's help and blessings."

Bino asked Jun to come to his bedside and told him, with his right hand tightly clasping his son's arm, "Son, seeing me in this predicament, you are now taking my place as the man of the family. You are having a man's role in a young boy's body. I put my trust and confidence in you."

Those words fortified Jun's spirit and will. He assured his father and mother that he was well prepared to take over as the man of the family.

Bino, despite his stroke, had the proper frame of mind. He was known as a strong-willed man. He always reminded himself, "In due time, I shall walk again. I shall walk again; and with God's help, I shall walk again. When the war ends and there is peace on earth again, I shall go back to teaching and be productive and gainfully employed."

Those words were recanted in his mind day in and day out. They were words of determination and comfort to him. In this regard, he asked a carpenter to bore holes through the walls of his bedroom with a drill. Through those holes, a large manila rope was tightly strung across his bedroom. He would struggle very hard to hold the rope and would painfully but patiently take some steps. That was his exercise four times a day for twenty minutes each time. He meticulously did this exercise every day.

He was aware that what he was doing would build up and strengthen muscles in his limbs and in his upper body. He was determined to walk again, to be able to run away from the Japanese, and ultimately to teach after the war was over.

Jun's cousin, Dr. Claire, a physician who stayed with their family during the war, was Bino's untiring physical therapist. After each exercise session, Dr. Clare would massage Bino's limbs and arms. Each session of therapy lasted for about forty-five minutes, which also assuaged the aching muscles and prevented them from being permanently atrophied. It was a great relief to Bino. He always told his niece, "You are really heaven sent to me." That was one way of expressing his gratitude to her.

One morning, Jun was surprised to see a great change in his father's countenance. If he were a bird, he would be chirping or singing like a lark. One of his visitors might have spilled the greatest news. Clandestine radios kept on broadcasting news for the consumption of those who were taking the risk and keeping their candles burning until the Americans returned.

Bino came to know, from the underground, that the spectacular Japanese victory over the United States and its allies during the last two years had been slipping from the palms of the rising sun. From island to island in the Pacific, the USAFE was reaping victories while the Japanese Imperial Forces were experiencing withdrawals.

In June 1944, the radio news further stated that General MacArthur's forces had landed in the northern part of Papua New Guinea, which is a stone's throw from the Philippines. The broadcast further continued, "This is the initial great offensive step towards the fulfillment of General Macarthur's promise to the Filipinos, 'I shall return.'"

At the same time, the radio newscast stated, "In the Central Pacific, the Japanese fleet and naval units experienced their most stunning defeat, particularly in the Philippine Sea."

In addition, it further stated, "The U.S. Marines annihilated the Japanese forces in Saipan." The significance was that it was an island within a bombing range of Japan and could be used as a U.S. airbase. All those developments gave intense joy to Bino and his family.

No wonder the Japanese soldiers in Badoc had been scanning the skies for possible intrusion of U.S. warplanes and looking beyond the wide horizon of the China Sea for U.S. naval ships.

Chapter 12

August to December 1944

On August 1, 1944, news from the radio reached Bino's home. "President Quezon, the president of the exiled Philippine government died in the United States." Jun saw his mother sitting beside Bino's bed with her hand seemingly shaking. He glanced at both of them, and there was a bereaved look in their faces.

Jun inquired, "Dad, are you in deep pain?"

Bino replied, "No, but I have some bad news. Our President Quezon died."

Jun saw tears welling in her mother's eyes. Fely had been very fond of the first lady, Aurora Quezon. Her legacy to the world was women's suffrage. President Quezon had the greatest support to uplift the rights of women.

It should be noted that women had been allowed to vote in the Philippines since 1935. Fely worked with Mrs. Quezon, together with Pilar Hidalgo Lim and Josefa Eascoda, the two ladies who were pillars of women's rights in the Philippines, propagating women's suffrage.

Fely was one of the leaders in advocating women's rights in the province of Ilocos Norte. She was in charge of adult education in the province. She went from barrio to barrio, from town to town, campaigning and pleading with the people, especially men, to support the rights of women.

She summoned old ladies to learn to read and write so that they could vote and exercise their right to choose their government leaders. Only those who could read and write were allowed to vote.

Jun, because of his fear of darkness, used to recollect those dark nights when he was practically tied to the skirt of her mother while she was teaching old women how to read and write. Their living room became the venue of elderly women learning civics and the three Rs.

While Fely would speak in public, advocating the rights of women, Jun would hear men jeering and shouting at her, "Wear pants in your home, not skirts."

Fely just scoffed at those remarks. She would make a joking remark at them, "We women are all united. Beware; sooner or later, you will be wearing skirts."

Bino gave all the encouragement and support he could give to his wife. Fely's hard work was rewarded when all those people she taught how to read and write were able to exercise their right to vote. She was most happy to know that she was able to uplift many women in her town and province from the darkness of illiteracy to the resplendent world of knowledge and wisdom.

Since then, women were equal to men in the Philippines. This was evidenced by women at the helm of the judiciary, the legislative body, and the executive branch of the government. They also found their niche in all the professions in the arts and sciences, especially in careers aside from law and medicine—which were only occupied by men—as engineers, airline pilots, and deck officers in merchant marine.

The news of the death of President Quezon really brought a spell of dismay to the Filipinos, in particular the guerrillas. The people had loved him so much.

To make up for their loss, the guerrillas were motivated to overrun the garrison in Badoc. One night during the first week of August, four men softly knocked at the door of Bino's house. Bino, sitting on his butaca, asked Jun to see who was on the porch. Jun pried open the door about half an inch. Recognizing one of them, he let them come in, and they were politely received.

Hurriedly, for fear of being seen or recognized, they told Bino, "By order of our commanding officer, evacuate within three days time. This will give you ample time to choose your evacuation place. Let it be known, in the veil of secrecy, to you and your close relatives, that prior to the landing of the Americans, which will be soon, we in the underground movement have to pave the way for the return of General MacArthur. There will soon be a general offensive from our end."

With those words spoken, they gave their final instructions to all the members of the family. "Inasmuch as Bino cannot walk yet, a horse will be waiting for him and Jun in barrio Bang-banga." This was chosen as a stepping stone for the whole family to go to their final evacuation place.

They further instructed Bino and his family, "You can tell people that you are going to the seaside, a restful place where the salt water and the warmth of the sandy beach on a sunny day could give you a therapeutic effect. This could be a very valid and credible reason, which will avoid any suspicion. One thing more: one of us will help you and your family find the way to your evacuation place."

They then bade them good-bye and wished them good luck.

The privilege extended them was in recognition of the services Jun and his family gave to the underground.

At the same time and day, another group went to the town mayor, Dr. Gus, ordering him and his family to evacuate within three days. They told him, "By order of our commander-in-chief of the Guerrilla Forces of Northern Luzon, you are hereby authorized to establish a military municipal government of Badoc, with full recognition of and full authority vested upon it by the USAFE. Your headquarters will be mobile to elude the Japanese Imperial Forces."

Bino had already made a mental picture of how they could reach Capandanan through Bang-banga.

On the third day, they were all set. They brought all the necessities that they thought would be useful and greatly needed while they were in the evacuation place. On their way to Bang-banga, it was the usual custom of the people to inquire, "Where are you going?" as a greeting. This phrase was more used than the words good morning, good afternoon, or good evening.

Fely would answer, "We are going to Bang-banga for a therapeutic treatment for Bino. The warmth of the sand and salt water and air could be good for Bino." It was common knowledge during those days that such an environment would be good for people who had a stroke. Therefore, there was no iota of suspicion that they were evacuating. People also knew that Fely's parents had some farms and properties near the sea. These gave them a feeling of great relief, as if a heavy burden had been lifted from their shoulders.

They finally arrived in Bang-banga. They stayed with one of their tenants named Immong. He was like a member of the family; hence, they felt at home there.

To avoid further suspicion, they lazed under the sun, went body surfing in the sea, or did some crabbing or gathered seashells. Time was their fortune. They took advantage of it before they had to once again run for their safety.

After a number of days, after dinnertime and under cover of darkness, a runner appeared with a horse. Everybody in Jun's family was ready to move at any moment's notice. As soon as the runner gave the signal to move, the whole family bade Immong good-bye and told him, "Till we meet again."

There was always an element of uncertainty during those days, whether people would meet again. They lived one day at a time. An hour or two could make the difference between life and death. It was wartime. Life might be snatched away by a bullet or by a stroke of a sword. Everybody was cognizant of this precarious situation.

Before proceeding to Capandanan, Jun approached his father and mother and told them his plans. He told them, "I have made a decision, like any able bodied man. I plan to join the guerrillas. I am leaving you behind and will be joining Dr. Lumang, a veterinarian, who was a Bataan veteran. I shall report to the mayor's headquarters. You will be hearing from me from time to time."

Fely did not approve of Jun's plan. However, Bino, having been a World War I veteran and having seen action in the Atlantic, paused and remained silent for quite some time, but held his composure. While Fely was almost hysterical from hearing Jun's decision, Bino remained calm. After Bino pacified Fely and assured her that everything would be all right, he told Jun, "Son, I am very proud of you. I am sure God will give you His blessings and protect you wherever you are. Find time to let us know how you are faring. Never forget to say your prayers, especially your holy rosary."

With those words spoken, Bino summoned Jun, hugged him tightly, and told him, "Remember your mama and your brother and sisters always. We love you, son. God bless you!" Jun kissed his mom, sisters, and brother, and his cousin, Dr. Claire.

Jun's parting words were, "It will not be long. War will soon end. We shall all be together again as one big family."

Without turning back, as their hearts were heavy over leaving Jun behind, they started their journey to Capandanan.

With the help of the runner and Immong, Bino was lifted with their bare arms to help him mount the horse. It was an ordeal for him. While Jun stood and bade them adieu again, the rest of the family followed the horse, with Bino astride. The runner held the reins of the horse, directing the way. They had to walk in single file, as the trail would allow only two to three people abreast to go through.

Their personal belongings were carried and balanced on the heads of the women. That was how women would carry heavy things in the Philippines. The runner, with an improvised sledge made out of two bamboo poles tied and attached to the sides of the saddle, placed the other personal effects of the family crisscrossed at the middle of the two parallel bamboo poles.

The trail was winding, following the riverbanks. Like in any rural area in the Philippines, during those years before extensive structural developments took place, the trail was lined on both sides with trees, foliage, and thick bushes. Because they walked by night, their first one hundred steps were severe tests of their mettle. They groped in the dark. They stumbled. They picked up things in the dark when personal belongings carried on their heads fell. Clearance from branches of trees hanging across the trail was low and could not be seen in the dark. For this reason, Bino had to stoop in a prone position on the saddle, with his arms around the neck of the horse. The low-hanging twigs and branches caught the burdens on the women's heads. This caused things to fall from their heads. Abrasions on their skin were painfully felt and were caused by rough branches of thorny bushes and dried twigs protruding from the sides of the narrow trail. They had to get used to the darkness, like banging one's head against a blank wall, and had to look out the corners of their eyes to allow them slight night vision.

There was fear plaguing them, as if there were Japanese soldiers lurking in the dark, ready to pounce upon them and bring them back to town for interrogation and torture.

When they neared the national highway, which they had to cross, darkness began to be enveloped by the dawn's early light. The runner ordered everybody to keep still; he heard motor engine noises. The hands of the runner restrained the horse by tightening his grip on the ropes. It did not make a move. Luckily, Bino, on horseback, was hidden by the thick trees, bushes, and under brushes that lined the trail, while the rest were in a crouching position.

Peeping through the bushes, the runner counted about four trucks in the convoy. They had to wait for another twenty minutes to make sure that there were no more trucks that would go by. The runner told everybody to make a dash. Everybody did, including the horse with Bino on the saddle, pulling the improvised sledge. This was the most terrifying moment. They took the risk, but the risk was worthwhile. They took a deep breath and heaved a great sigh of relief. They made it to the safety of the mountains and forests on the other side of the national highway.

Their eyes were heavy due to lack of sleep. Their legs tired and spirits weary, they had to take a short rest.

As the sun rose over the Cordillera ranges, the whole family continued to move, but as slow as a swamp turtle. When they saw some barns on the way and some goats grazing in the open fields, Bino said, "We are now nearing our destination, our temporary home."

Unwittingly, they were already there. They only realized they had arrived in their destination when a farmer leading a cow to graze in the fields told them when queried, "You are now in Capandanan."

The runner inquired where the barrio capitan was. He directed them to the barrio capitan's house. His name was Jose. He came down from his house and was surprised to see Bino and his family.

He welcomed them with utmost sincerity. Briefly, they exchanged greetings and pleasantries, and then he led them up to his house. They helped Bino dismount from the horse, carried him up the bamboo stairs, and propped him up in a deep sofa made out of rattan with soft cotton cushions.

Jose's whole family came to the living room. The children were introduced one by one to each member of Bino's family. Jose's wife, Ittang, excused herself. She went to the kitchen, detached from the house and only connected by a catwalk, to prepare breakfast.

While waiting for breakfast to be served, Jose and Bino had a brief time to remember their childhood days. They used to be playmates and classmates in grade school. They only parted ways when both went to high school in different towns.

While a very young schoolboy, Jose stayed with his uncle, who was married to Bino's aunt. The affinity between the two made everybody very comfortable with one another. This made things much easier for the evacuees.

While savoring breakfast, Jose told Bino that he had found a place for them, a real hideaway. He was like a salesman promoting the evacuation place. He told Bino, "You will like it. It is a very rustic but picturesque place, situated along a creek, in between hills that are heavily forested. The hut is twelve feet by sixteen feet and is very ideal for the whole family, but with some discomfort. The floor is made out of bamboo slats about an inch wide, arranged and pieced together. It is raised about three feet from the ground in front, and about five feet at the rear, since the ground gradually slanted towards the creek. A buri mat can be placed on the bamboo floor to simulate a carpet."

The water in the creek was clear and apparently pure. It sprung from a mountain ridge and dropped as a waterfall and flowed downwards, winding its way towards the hideaway.

He forewarned them, "To cook, use your imagination. Extinguish the fire immediately once you hear the drone of airplanes. Never cook at night, as the cinders and the fire could betray your whereabouts. Even during daytime, beware of the smoke that curls up into the sky."

He continued giving his lecture, like a scoutmaster to a tenderfoot scout. "In order to have a safe drinking water, build a well beside the creek. Place a lot of pebbles at the bottom and sides as water filters, and wait for the water to ooze from the bottom and sides. Once the small well is filled with water, scoop the water with a dipper and pour it into a boiling pot. Boil the water and let it cool off overnight. You will have a very safe drinking water for sure.

"To bathe yourselves," he continued, "go downstream. There is a spot as wide as a junior Olympic-sized swimming pool where water accumulates and then trickles down again into another creek. The depth is about four to five feet, which is like a lap swimming pool. You will enjoy taking a dip during hot weather."

Jose finally helped Bino to mount his horse and led everybody to their new hideaway. On their way, Jose explained about the medicinal herbs that were growing wild in the mountains. Those were within one's reach whenever one got sick. The medical doctor, Dr. Claire, could give her expertise in botany and pharmacology. She could decide what herbs to use and the dosage. For instance, there were lots of cinchona trees growing wild in the forests, the bark of which, when brewed until it reaches the color of tea, is a good cure of malaria. The extract is quinine.

They finally arrived at their hideaway, and it gave them nostalgic thoughts of the past, when the kids were going camping as boy scouts and campfire girls and Bino was the scoutmaster.

Once Bino's family was encamped in the evacuation hideaway, Jun and Dr. Lumang left on their way from Bang-banga to the mayor's headquarters. They were like batons handed down by a runner to the hands of subsequent runners in a relay team, until they reached the finish line, the mayor's headquarters.

Immediately, they reported to the mayor, Dr. Gus, who received them politely. Unknown to the mayor, Dr. Lumang, also not knowing his situation, was already a marked or doomed man. All those guerrillas from Ilocos Norte, namely Captain Monje, Captain Madamba, and Lt. Magno and their respective men, were similarly marked men. A new guerrilla outfit was also formed with Lt. In-niong as the commander; he was also a Bataan veteran. This lieutenant, a very competent man, was also from Badoc. But his outfit was also doomed.

The other guerrilla faction from Ilocos Sur, which encroached on Ilocos Norte, was greater in numbers and more armed. They wanted to rule the whole Ilocos region. As a ploy, they invited all the guerrilla forces from Ilocos Norte to a meeting and party to come to an agreement that they should all be one for a common cause. The Ilocos Norte guerrillas thought that this would be a very good agreement and plan. They were most happy thinking that they would all be fighting together. By the theory of strength in numbers, they thought they could annihilate the Japanese soldiers in the Ilocos region. To them, that would be a great opportunity.

On the other hand, the other faction from Ilocos Sur had bad intentions. They let the barrio people prepare food for the banquet. Pigs, cattle, goats, and chicken were slaughtered and prepared under different menus.

Similarly, fish, shrimp, and fresh water clams, which were abundant in the river, were caught and prepared nicely, with all the trimmings, for the occasion.

Desserts made out of rice flour and shredded coconuts and sweetened with molasses, then wrapped with banana leaves, were steamed. These were served piping hot on the table.

Flowers from the mountains were arranged for the party and set on the tables as if done by a professional interior decorator.

It was a banquet set in the open air. When the table was ready, Captain Dionie announced, "Everybody be seated in your designated places. Dinner is now served. Please be seated." Everyone sat.

They fully appreciated all the dishes with the local alcoholic beverage, basi. The guerrillas from Ilocos Norte thought they were being wined and dined by their fellow guerrillas from Ilocos Sur. They had that great feeling of well-being and pleasure, thinking that they were recipients of hospitality by the Ilocos Sur faction.

Since the Badoc guerrillas were very naïve about the inner motives of the opposing guerrillas, their rifles were stacked together in a military fashion before the banquet. All their side arms were neatly placed on one table, showing their absolute certainty in the trustworthiness of the opposing guerrillas.

The Badoc guerrillas were inebriated by the basi. The opportune time for the opposing guerrillas had come. Their commander gave the signal.

The Ilocos Norte guerrillas became easy prey. The opposing guerrillas herded the Ilocos Norte guerrillas like cattle, and according to information, they were led to an undisclosed killing field. After the war, they were never seen again.

Chapter 13
Critical Days of Badoc

During this period, the guerrillas from Ilcocos Sur were already in control of all the barrios in Ilocos Norte, which were governed by civilians appointed by the guerrillas.

In the town of Badoc, there were people who did not evacuate. They did not trust the guerrillas for fear that women would be raped and men would be summarily executed. They were domiciled in the Catholic church. Each family built their own cubicles inside the church for privacy. They set their own beds and pieces of furniture as they would in their respective houses. The size of the cubicle was in proportion to the size of the family.

The Catholic priest, Father Florentino, stayed with his flock. He honestly believed that it was his obligation to minister to them. After all, the church was under him and the people in the church were his parishioners. Many of those who stayed behind and lived in the church were close relatives and friends of Bino and Fely's family. Many of them were close friends, cousins, aunts, and uncles, either by consanguinity or by spiritual affinity.

Jun was adversely affected emotionally. His love, Chita, was left behind in town. To assuage his aching soul, he entertained a make believe situation where Chita was always at his side. This way he could subjectively commune with her and be close to her. Only in dreams did he hold her.

All those left behind in town were all marked as pro-Japanese by the guerrillas and the bolo men. They were the living dead. Those in town were cognizant of their situation. For this reason, they also armed themselves and organized their own vigilante groups. But they could not defend themselves because they were few in numbers. It should be noted that not one of them was pro-Japanese as construed by the guerrillas and the bolo men. They were hoping against hope that they would survive the war. They knew that their only chance to see the end of the war was for the Americans to liberate them from the claws of the Japanese and from the wrath of the guerrillas and bolo men.

There was a *balitang cochero* (rumor) circulating within the confines of their own circle in church that the Americans were already hopping from island to island in the South Pacific—such as Iwo Jima, Saipan, Wake Island, etc.—and that General MacArthur was on his way to liberate the Philippines.

The invasion of Saipan left the corridors of Japan, Formosa, and the Philippines open for air strikes and, ultimately, invasion. This was a great morale booster to them—their only hope. They indulged in dwelling upon this news. They hung on, hoping that the Americans would be able to liberate them and protect them from their three-pronged enemies, namely the guerrillas, the bolo men, and the Japanese.

At this stage of the war, Jun clerked for the municipal mayor. Their headquarters was in a very remote place hidden in the Cordillera Mountains. He typed military orders, information for the people, for implementation. Such orders were at times incredible and quixotic. For instance, Jun typed a circular that stated, "Anybody caught by the Japanese alive is considered a spy; hence, he will be executed." The rationale, according to Dr. Gus et al., was that it was the belief of the guerrillas that anybody interrogated and tortured would divulge information to the Japanese about where the guerrillas were. In view of all those developments, civilians, especially from the town, were already resigned to their fate. The Japanese soldiers were also suspicious of them, and the guerrillas and bolo men shared the same conviction.

The Japanese soldiers intensified their mopping up operations, and at the same time, gathered food and harvested rice and maize in the farms. Those unharvested crops were abandoned. Whatever food they brought to town, they also shared with those entrenched in the church.

Once the Japanese went out, the runners conked their bamboo tubes, as noted earlier, and relayed the message that the Japanese were on their way. The guerrillas would then go deeper and deeper into the mountains, while the civilians who were left behind had to fend for themselves. The guerrillas did not protect them, but the civilians protected the guerrillas by sealing their lips about where the guerrillas and ammunitions were.

Coming out from their hiding places, the guerrillas would order the civilians to slaughter animals for food, prepare food for them fit for a king, and choose beautiful girls to massage their bodies. Dr. Gus, the mayor, knew that this was one of his headaches. But he was weak and scared of the guerrillas; hence, he tolerated this vice.

On the other hand, Mayor Perto of the neighboring town, Pinili, who was married to Fely's first cousin, did not allow this to happen in his municipality. At one time, the guerrillas tried to do this in his municipality. He barked at them, "Over my dead body; you cannot do this thing in my own town. We can feed you the way we feed our own people but never abuse young girls. You should be the ones to protect them as your own sisters."

They obeyed and respected him. They knew that he had a backbone. The bolo men in his own town gave him their utmost support.

After some months of working in the military mayor's office, Jun was curious about where Dr. Lumang was. He thought that he was already installed as one of the officers in the guerrilla movement in view of his being a war veteran in Bataan. He did not know that Dr. Lumang became one of the statistics, executed by the other guerrilla faction. They thought he was a die-hard member of the Monje, Madamba, and Magno guerrilla faction. They considered him an intruder.

The military mayor, Dr. Gus, called Jun to go to his office. Jun saluted the mayor, and he told Jun to be seated. The mayor broke the news to Jun. "Your companion, Dr. Lumang, was summarily executed the other day."

Jun was speechless. He felt as if his blood had completely drained from his body. His knees were about to buckle with fright. With an authoritarian voice, the mayor commanded Jun, "Go back to your parents for your own protection. The guerrillas know that you came here with Dr. Lumang. Go immediately, without any delay."

The mayor added, "I cannot protect you from the guerrillas."

This was incredible. He knew Jun since childhood, as he was their family physician. For this reason, Jun thought, the mayor could protect him from the guerrillas. Instead, Jun judged him as a person without any spinal column, a very weak man.

With those words spoken earlier, Jun followed the mayor's order without any great delay and proceeded to go to his family's hideaway.

Jun was relayed from runner to runner. On his way to Capandanan, he took a rest in Barrio Napu. The capitan del barrio, named Ago, requested Jun to rest in his house while his wife prepared lunch for him. Jun expressed his gratitude to him and his wife for their kindness and generosity. At that moment, Jun saw a lady whose profile was turned towards him. She seemed very familiar.

Jun approached her. True enough, she was the first cousin of his father. She was Auntie Victoria. She wondered what brought Jun to this place, Napu. When Jun sat beside her, she whispered into his ears with tears streaming down her cheeks, "Your uncle, Magno, is already gone. He was one of those massacred at that banquet where he was invited to join the opposing guerrillas." Jun knew this as he heard the news while he was working in the mayor's office.

After lunch, an old man was brought before a crowd. His face was badly beaten and battered, with blood already caked over his hair and face. Jun recognized him immediately, despite his face being disfigured. This was Jun's granduncle, Marcelo, the father of Lt. Magno. He was led by one of the bolo men with his hands tied behind his back. He was like a cattle led to the slaughter.

One of the bolo men told him, "We will spare your life if you can tell us where your son, Lt. Magno, hid his cache of ammunitions and firearms."

The poor old man could not give any reply because he actually did not know where they were. They repeated the same query over and over, but he could not give any reply. In front of Jun, someone took a medium-sized sword, thrust it into Marcelo's left shoulder blade, and then gave the fatal blow, a stab towards his chest. Blood spurted from the wounds. He collapsed in due time, apparently in great agony until he breathed his last.

Jun was so paralyzed with fright that no tears welled from his eyes. His great grief dried the oasis of tears from his eyes. With all the tortures and executions Jun had witnessed, either he was already immune or his feelings were no longer sensitive to such happenings. He had reached the saturation point. He became like a zombie. At that very moment, he could no longer feel the pangs of sorrow.

Jun finally reached Capandanan. He sought the capitan del barrio, Jose, to help him find his parents. He did not know the hideaway of his parents. Jun had known Jose since he met him several times when he went to supervise the harvesting of rice in that barrio. Upon arrival, Fely inquired, "What happened?" She knew something went wrong as indicated by Jun's face, which was still pale. His eyes showed signs of fear. His voice was still quavering. The trauma caused by what he experienced in Napu was absolutely visible, evidenced by his physical appearance. Jun related to his parents what he saw. Bino and Fely were also greatly shaken.

News circulated in the Philippines that General Yamashita, the Tiger of Malaysia, was given an immediate new assignment from his exile in Manchuria to take command of the Japanese forces in the Philippines.

Several books and reports indicated that General Yamashita was known as a very intelligent individual, amiable, courteous, and very popular both in the ranks and in the higher ranks. He had a strong mind, and was clean, full of integrity, and kind, with a good sense of humor. He was Premier Tojo's archrival; hence, it was believed he was transferred to Manchuria after his great victory in the then Malayan Peninsula. He was responsible for the defeat of the British forces in Singapore, which was considered at that time to be a fortress as impregnable as the Maginot Line.

The British armada and fleet protected Singapore from assault by sea. But he conquered it. Historians said that he could have been the minister of war. He was slated for that position, but politics sent him to the Philippines.

While in the Philippines, General Yamashita was not happy at all with his assignment. He did not know the Philippine conditions. He was not cognizant of the conditions of the Japanese forces or the supply of ammunitions and other war requisites. He knew that his assignment was rather difficult and doomed to failure. What he learned in Tokyo during his briefing was not to his liking, as he was aware of the imminent threat of the American forces.

He had a terrible premonition. Those who were near his family said that when he flew to Manila in October 1944, his wife, with bleary and teary eyes, knew that that would be the last time she would see him again. Similarly, General Yamashita shared this same apprehension about his wife.

One morning on October 10, 1944, clandestine radio in Badoc announced that Halsey's carriers started to attack Luzon. For three to four successive days, reports indicated that the line of American attacks were from Luzon to Okinawa and Formosa. During those days, a display of American sea and airpower was in action. It was said that hundreds of American warplanes were in full combat.

About 10:00 a.m. on the same day, the sky over Ga-ang Port in Ilocos Norte was filled with twin-bodied fighter planes (the P-38 planes), mustangs, bombers, and single-motored small liaison planes. The number of U.S. planes hovering, diving, and releasing their bombs were numerous, because their shadows cast on the ground covered a large area of Capandanan.

The port that was bombarded was less than twenty kilometers away from the hideaway of Bino and his family. Looking at the skies, Jun saw the Japanese zeros engaged in dogfights with the American fighter planes. He had to seek cover in the creek, but raised his head from time to time to look at the dogfights.

The Japanese anti-aircraft guns opened up, like gray puffs dotting the skies. American planes strafed and dropped their bombs on Japanese ships that laid anchor at Ga-ang Port. Thick smoke billowed from the explosions that disabled and sunk the Japanese ships, and it could be seen miles and miles away.

People danced and shouted with glee, oblivious of the dangers of stray bullets from above and from the sea. The sight of the skies was overwhelming. People knew then that liberation of the Philippines had finally come.

Captain Ueda, who was once the garrison commander of Badoc, personally went to Badoc from Laoag after the bombing of Ga-ang Port, telling people in the town and nearby barrios to "Run for your lives. Seek cover in a more secure area. The Americans are coming."

Those words obviously showed how he cared for the people who once held him in high esteem. There was still goodness inherent in him despite being an enemy of the Filipinos. People were grateful to him, in absentia, as he might have saved some lives during their retreat towards Manila. Those who were caught during their retreat were treated badly or executed on the spot. They could not be blamed, as any able-bodied man at that time might have been a guerrilla or a bolo man. It could have meant the lives of the Japanese.

Those left behind in Badoc, entrenched in the church, were cowering with great fear. Even physically, they were like wet chicken. After the bombing of Ga-ang Port, the Japanese regrouped in Laoag, Ilocos Norte, to defend the Gabu Airport, which was just at the fringe of Laoag. However, they had nothing to defend, as all the Japanese airplanes and hangars at the Gabu Airport were destroyed and in shambles. This was a cause for alarm for the civilians left behind in Badoc. They knew that they were just as good as dead. They were the so-called wanted people or the marked men.

Guerrillas and bolo men were then free as the wind to go to town. They herded all those people living in the church, separated the children and the elderly from the men, both young and old, and isolated the young women from the elderly.

The death march of the people who lived in the church started after the Japanese left the town. They were paraded from barrio to barrio, with their hands tied behind their backs, until they reached the killing fields. They were jeered at by the bolo men, struck by the sides of the bolos or by bamboo poles on any parts of their bodies, or stabbed by small knives, making sure that only a centimeter of the blade would penetrate the skin to cause a slow and painful death. Those methods were used to inflict intense and prolonged pain. People who saw them did not show their grief. They were crying in the inside, careful not to show any public display of sympathy. Otherwise, they would reveal their true feelings and be the next one to be tortured as a sympathizer.

Regardless of age—from thirteen years of age to the ages of senior citizens—they were tortured and finally executed. There were more than two hundred adult males tortured and put to death, including teenaged males and senior citizens. Many were friends, close relatives, and acquaintances of Bino's family.

Reports indicated that the late Father Florentino, well respected and loved by the parishioners before and during the war, was severely tortured by the bolo men. They cut off one of his ears and let him chew it before they gave him the final thrust of the sword into his heart. Those who witnessed his execution said that he endured the pains with Christ-like acceptance. He murmured prayers for the forgiveness of the perpetrators.

Parents, before they were tortured to death, saw their sons being executed first. Fathers, before their execution, saw their daughters being abused by the bolo men.

Chita's fate was much better than most of the young girls in the group. A young guerrilla officer, Lt. Tinio, got a glimpse of her while the young girls were lined up. The young officer knew her parents. Chita's father was a prominent physician in Ilocos Norte. But like any other males taken from the church, he was bludgeoned to death, together with his son. Lt. Tinio took her. He let her stay with his sister.

While under the protection of the young lieutenant, Chita sent a message to Jun through the runners. In that message, she conveyed to Jun, "Please come and rescue me. This is to let you know that I am waiting for you to bring me to your place. If you really care for me, despite what happened, snatch me from an undesirable situation."

The message, though, was handed to Bino. At that time, Jun was down with malaria, a sickness transmitted by mosquitoes. Not wanting to add insult to injury, Bino never handed the message to Jun. Bino also thought of one reason to keep the message a secret and not divulge it to Jun. Instead, he let Fely read the message. She could not utter any words. She, being a woman, could understand Chita's predicament. Bino and Fely discussed this without the presence of anybody else.

Bino made this comment to Fely, "Our son is a mere child. He is barely sixteen years old. Chita is one year younger. I will not let them live as husband and wife without the benefit of the sacrament of matrimony. They are too young to get married."

Fely added, "I fully agree with you. Furthermore, they have to finish high school and go to college after the war. If they live together now, without the benefit of a church wedding, they will be living in sin. One thing more, they are not yet responsible, and they are too young to bring up a child, especially at wartime. They think only of the bliss of being together. At their ages, they can be prolific. Considering the number of reproductive years ahead of them, they could have many tiny guests arrive in their nest. How can they support a large family?"

Those were Bino's and Fely's concerns. For this reason, Bino kept the message. He only told Jun, "Chita is very safe. She is now in Pinili.

She is in the safe hands of the family of Lt. Tinio. She is now staying with them"

Jun heard the message. He was most happy for the deliverance of Chita from harm. Immediately, Jun told his parents, "I have to fulfill my promise. I told her I will have her in life till the end of time. I have to go and bring her home."

As Bino discerned Jun's great determination to bring Chita home and marry her when the war ended, he said with endearment, "Son, you are very sick. You cannot go. In the meantime, you should rationalize things. Wait till the war is over. If you will still love her, then follow your plans."

Bino and Fely were careful not to show a negative attitude; otherwise, Jun would pursue his plans. Immediately after the war, Jun came to know that the young lieutenant and Chita learned to love each other and finally got married. After a year, they had a bouncing baby boy.

The execution of more than two hundred men, young and old, was an incident that cannot be forgotten. The story of the massacre was handed down from the previous to the present generation. People cannot forget those heinous crimes committed against humanity during the war. On the other hand, as years went by, the families, relatives, and friends of the victims opened up their hearts to forgive the wicked, whose hands perpetrated those crimes. There was closure.

Chapter 14

"I shall return ... I have returned"

From February 8 to 9, 1942, General Douglas MacArthur, on his way to Australia, promised, "I shall return." Those were the rallying words of the Filipinos. Those words strengthened their faith in the United States. When spirits reached their lowest, the general's famous words buoyed them up throughout the war years and enabled them to ride out on the crest to victory.

On October 19, 1944, the general spent his night on board the cruiser, *Nashville*. It was reported that he slept well that night, as dead as a log. Before dawn could bring its early light in October 20, it was reported that the general woke up early, as sprightly as can be and as chirpy as a lark. While dressing and preparing for breakfast, nostalgia set upon him. He had a flashback. According to reports, his aide heard him say in a murmur, "Forty years ago, I stood here in Leyte as a young officer."

In that early morning, he took his breakfast. After that, he took his corncob pipe in between his well-sculptured lips, lit it, and smoked, with the aroma of the pipe tobacco lightly carried by the wind, overpowering the salty smell of the sea. He majestically strode onto the bridge. Therein, he witnessed the first wave of American soldiers who landed at the beach of Leyte. On the basis of this first assault, he envisioned a victory beyond his expectations. His heart thumped with triumph as he saw the G-Is chomping at the bit to get to the shore, with great success. He was greatly elated by the feat achieved by the 24th Division. At that moment, it was said that he was wrapped up with an exaggerated feeling of well-being and pleasure.

As described by Stanley L. Falk in his *Decision at Leyte*, General MacArthur donned a fresh uniform, wore his famous MacArthur sunglasses with his familiar gold-braided headgear, and regally walked on the deck. A barge below the deck was full of officers and newspapermen, including the Philippine President Sergio Osmena and Brig. General Carlos P. Romulo. It should be noted that General Romulo was a Pulitzer Prize winner before World War II; and he later became the President of the University of the Philippines and later on the Secretary of Foreign Affairs of the Government of the Philippines. At one time, he was the President of the General Assembly of the United Nations.

A ladder was laid down to the barge waiting below, and he took measured steps to go down the ramp. They moved with the crest and troughs of the waves rushing to the shore. Emotions also rode high amongst the passengers. General MacArthur at that very moment was described as being "like a high school student with his first date at his first prom." He was heard telling General Sutherland, his chief of staff, "It is unbelievable; we are here now in Leyte."

Several yards away from the shore, the barge came to a standstill. The ramp was set down in about a foot of water. The general went down. His feet felt the safety of the ground, waded, and happily moved with a low, slapping sound made by his boots and legs where the waves broke on the shore. Newspapermen, officers, and aides followed him, along with

President Sergio Osmena. Despite the precarious situation where they were treading, smiles were seen and soft laughter was heard when they saw General Romulo following the entourage with the water level up to his waist or with the level of the crest of the waves up to his armpit or neck. He was less than five feet three inches tall. This picture was caught when the cameras of the war reporters were whirring, recording the most historic scene of World War II, the famous Landing of Leyte.

Having set his right foot ashore on the beach of Leyte, he hurriedly went inland to inspect whatever damages were inflicted by the recent explosions of bombs, salvos from the U.S. Navy ships, and the artillery. Dangers still lurked beyond where the general was supposed to advance. Japanese artillery continued to direct a barrage of mortar and canon salvos on the landing areas. Stray bullets fired from Japanese small firearms were still within the ambit where the general strode. It was like skating in an area of thin ice above a deep blue sea. He was aware of the perilous situation, but because of his great desire to announce his return, he did not mind the dangers around him. He went back to the beach and grabbed a microphone that might have been set up either by the engineering corps or the signal corps. He spoke in a deep voice, with great emotion, fulfilling his promise of "I shall return" with "I have returned."

Those words echoed throughout the world. Those jubilantly hearing it on the clandestine radios in the Island of Luzon, in particular, the city of Manila, danced in place or jumped with joy upon hearing their great hero and idol. They were careful not to be seen publicly displaying their great emotions of joy by the soldiers of General Yamashita. People in Badoc knew they were already liberated not only from the Japanese but also from the guerrillas and bolo men.

The American soldiers landed thereafter in Northern Luzon and set up their headquarters in Laoag. Dr. Gus, the mayor, set up the government in Badoc. Once the people came to know that the municipal government of Badoc was set up in the town, they came down in exodus from their evacuation places. The Japanese soldiers from Ilocos Norte had a reverse position, vis-à-vis, the guerrillas. In turn, the Japanese hid in the cordilleras and in the mountains of Neuva Vizcaya. They joined the forces of General Yamashita. The Japanese became the hunted, and the guerrillas were the hunters.

Bino and all members of his family including Dr. Claire, his niece, and their helper, Concha, went back to town. They had great tasks to do: to help rebuild the whole town, a large part of which was razed to the ground by fire; to clean up the schools and churches, which were opened a few months after; to share and support one another; and to console those whose loved ones had been victims of the Japanese, the guerillas, and the bolo men.

In due time, the Battle of Manila in February 1945 took place. The American prisoners of war barricaded and imprisoned at the Universidad de Sto. Tomas were a pitiful sight, looking emaciated. Their skins tightly covered their bones, their ribs protruded from their sides, and their eyes were deeply sunken in their sockets. It was providential that they were liberated early.

On the other hand, during the last few days of the war, the Japanese wrought havoc in Manila, especially on civilians. They were bayoneted to death once caught on their paths of retreat. Pregnant women had their wombs pried open with bayonets; babies were tossed in the air only to be skewered once returned to earth by gravity. Those were some of the nauseating scenes seen during the retreat of the Japanese.

General Douglas MacArthur proclaimed, "The Philippines is now liberated." This was on that memorable day of July 5, 1945. Peace was most welcome in all corners of the Philippines. Church bells in Badoc rang exuberantly, announcing the coming of an era of peace and full of great promise. People ran in the streets and danced with joy. They hugged or kissed everybody that they met. Some also broke plates in their homes out of excitement. They became ecstatic. They were overwhelmed by the advent of a condition of supreme well-being and good spirits emanating from the victory of Uncle Sam in the Philippines.

Chapter 15

Reflections

After the war, people tried to forget and find closure for what transpired on those trying years. They simply wanted to go on with their lives. But that was easier said than done.

Jun still had those bad dreams and nightmares. Even more than sixty years after World War II, those horrifying experiences haunted him. However, he took advantage of those years that had gone by. They were his bounty. He was able to unwind himself and alleviate his condition. Occurrences of his bad dreams and nightmares became less frequent. They registered significant decrements as years rolled by.

He had to find closure. The first thing he did was to eradicate his sense of survivor's guilt. At the same time, he tried to free himself from the emotional pains caused by the untimely deaths of his classmates, playmates, friends, relatives, and acquaintances by the hands of the bolo men. This was achieved by forgiving those who trespassed against humanity. He mustered great courage and effort to do all those commendable acts. It should be noted that the act of forgiving is a manifestation of great strength on the part of the forgiver.

In attempting to meticulously reflect upon his war experiences, he became more aware of the positive aspects that emanated from the war. Jun was in his formative years during World War II. Whatever was positively absorbed during those years molded him into the man he is right now.

For instance, in his observations and experiences of what people of all walks of life did, made, thought, and said—including shared systems, attitudes, and feelings—Jun thought of the iceberg theory. This theory advances the belief that just as 90 percent of an iceberg is visible above the water line, there are also 90 percent of its attributes, attitudes, and values that are out of sight and submerged below the water line. Those are called the out-of-awareness attributes, attitudes and values. Those are the attributes in life that Jun had in retrospect and had in mind to discuss in his reflections.

The first one is self-reliance. This is the absolute certainty in the trustworthiness of oneself. Without it, survival during the war would have not been possible. As they say, "God helps those who help themselves."

He found out that despite the difficulties and sufferings people experienced during the war, they placed their hope and faith in God. They were like a drowning man who clings onto anything, even a straw that floats by, in an attempt to save himself. Their faith and hope in God never diminished. This was evidenced by the resilience of the Filipino people during World War II.

He discovered that there is always goodness in a man or in a woman, no matter how bad he or she is. For instance during the war, a well-known die-hard criminal in Jun's hometown saved a child from a burning house, endangering his own life. This man had been ostracized for a long time in his hometown. However, after this incident, his past became eclipsed by his heroic act.

Following the example above, a guerrilla in the Philippines was about to be executed by Japanese Military Police. People in the guerrilla movement knew the Japanese Military Police for inflicting torture and executions. When the guerrilla was about to be executed, the Japanese officer noted a glint from the chain of the guerrilla's necklace. That which glittered was the emblem of Free Masonry. Incidentally, the Japanese officer was a Free Mason. Despite their being enemies at wartime, the Japanese officer spared the life of the guerrilla and told him to flee and get lost.

Those examples showed that there is that innate nature of a person beyond his/her total self, wherein an element of goodness still prevails. One should always remember the adage, "One should be much slower to condemn, if need be, and faster to forgive."

Another positive aspect that one can draw from the war is sensitivity. Sensitivity to the innate nature of others and responding to them through empathy becomes imperative to understand others and to be understood. People from the cities evacuating in rural areas during the war learned how to adapt themselves by understanding the customs and traditions of the rural people. They exercised great sensitivity to the innate nature and the characteristics of their brothers in the rural areas. By doing so, they developed harmonious relationships with them. They understood their rural brothers; and in turn, they, too, were understood. This can also be transformed at present, with peoples of different customs and traditions in our community, through cultural awareness. We must wring out ethnocentricity if unity amongst divergent groups in a community will be achieved.

From the above, one can deduce that unity in diversity can be attained through the management of cultural differences.

Above all, Jun learned subjective Philippine family values. Even in the evacuation places, respect for the elderly was foremost.

The spirit of cooperation amongst people was also seen, even on the farms during the war. This was exemplified by the cooperative efforts of farmers in harvesting their produce or in building their houses. They helped one another without any pecuniary considerations. The symbiosis—the give and take—was always taken into account. This was greatly inculcated into Jun's moral fiber, not solely by his parents, but also by the customs and traditions of the people. This was validated during the war.

Politeness and hospitality were greatly shown during the war, which formed Jun's character. Even in far-flung areas, when one had no place to go to be exposed to the vagaries of nature, and no food to eat or water to drink, there were always hands ready, even from complete strangers, to give and to share. With open arms and open hearts, they received people, even those unknown to them.

From those observations, Jun came to learn that it is more blessed to give than to receive. Bread cast on the water comes back to you. The good deed you have sown today may benefit you or someone you love at a time when you least expect it.

What was practiced by Bino, Fely, and their family during the war was deeply ingrained in Jun and his family. That is, the family that prays together, stays together. They wished to propagate this practise. For what? For endless reasons. From it springs forth love and sharing. From it emanates respect, empathy, sensitivity, and all other family values. In short, it is the axis around which all the attitudes, values, and feelings revolve. It strengthens the family ties and holds the family together, no matter where they are and wherever they will be.

Reflecting, one at a time, on those experiences felt and observations made during World War II, Jun seriously perceived the miracles of prayer. Through it, transcendence occurred: from distrust to faith, from pain and sickness to miraculous cure, from despair to hope, from fear to fortitude, from sorrow to joy, and from death to belief in eternal life.

BIBLIOGRAPHY

Philippine Centennial Review, ***One Hundred Years of the Life of a Nation,*** Centennial Celebration of the Declaration of Philippine Independence, June 12, 1896 to June 12, 1998, Filipino Council of Southern Texas, Houston, TX., 1998

Falk, L. Stanley, ***Decision At Leyte,*** W. W. Norton & Company, Inc., New York, N.Y., 1966

Lacambra, Maria Jose, ***Rising Sun Blinking,*** Sinag – Tala Publishers Inc., Manila, Philippines, March 1995

Association of Badoquenos in California, ***Badoc, Ilocos Norte, A Brief Profile,*** First Anniversary Celebration, Souvenir Program, 1996

Republic of the Philippines, Province of Ilocos Norte, Municipality of Badoc, ***The Town Executives from 1764 to the present,*** Province of Ilocos Norte Printing Press, Laoag, Ilocos Norte, 1996.

Harris, Philip R. & Moran, Robert T, ***Managing Cultural Differences,*** Gulf Publishing Company, Houston, TX, 1987

About the Author

A United Nations Principal Officer (Retired) of the United Nations Economic and Social Commission for Asia and the Pacific; formerly an economist of the United Nations Food & Agriculture Organization and the Philippine Government; formerly a university professor in the Philippines and an Adjunct Faculty Staff of some universities in Texas; and author of various technical papers, studies and documents; a poet and a pianist; a community volunteer worker; and an independent international business consultant.

Printed in the United States
147593LV00002BB/12/P